OF KISSES & QUESTS

ALSO BY RACHEL MORGAN

CREEPY HOLLOW

The Faerie Guardian

The Faerie Prince

The Faerie War

A Faerie's Secret

A Faerie's Revenge

A Faerie's Curse

Glass Faerie

Shadow Faerie

Rebel Faerie

Of Kisses & Quests

CREEPY HOLLOW COMPANION NOVELLAS

Scarlett

Raven

RIDLEY KAYNE CHRONICLES

Elemental Thief

Elemental Power

Elemental Heir

CITY OF WISHES

The Complete Cinderella Story

A COLLECTION OF CREEPY HOLLOW STORIES

OF KISSES & QUESTS

RACHEL MORGAN

Epub ISBN 978-1-928510-44-4
Paperback ISBN 978-1-928510-45-1
Hardback ISBN 978-1-928510-46-8

www.rachel-morgan.com

To the Creepy Hollow superfans.
Thank you for loving these characters
as much as I do.

CONTENTS

GLOW-BUG BUTTS & MAGIC CARPETS

This story is Ryn's point of view of the magic carpet kiss scene from *The Faerie Prince*, long requested by many fans of the Creepy Hollow series.

Along with that particular scene and a few of the scenes leading up to it, you'll also get to read the story behind the *"I may have been six years old, but I haven't forgotten." / "Ah, yes. Our first and only kiss."* exchange between Ryn and Violet.

Read this story any time after *The Faerie Prince*, Creepy Hollow Book Two.

CHAPTER 1

About Twelve Years Ago

THE CARRIAGE SOARED ACROSS THE GLITTER-FILLED NIGHT SKY as Ryn Larkenwood, his feet bouncing back and forth against the lower part of the seat, continued scratching his arms.

"Ryn, stop fidgeting," his mother said.

"But this jacket is itchy."

"Reed's suit is exactly the same as yours, and he isn't fidgeting."

Ryn looked across the carriage at his older brother. Reed's eyes widened. He glanced at Mom, then back at Ryn, before grinning and scratching his arm. Ryn covered his mouth to smother his laughter.

Mom sighed. "That wasn't your cue to start misbehaving, Reed."

Dad looked away from the window and put his stern face on. "Have you two forgotten where we're going?"

"A party?" Ryn said.

"At a Guild Councilor's house?" Reed added.

"Correct. An important Guild Councilor. So you need to look

good when we get there. After you've been introduced, you can take the jackets off."

"Can we eat there?" Ryn asked.

"Of course you can eat," Mom said. "We don't expect you to go hungry."

"He means the grown-up food," Reed explained. "On the floating trays." He looked at Ryn, who nodded in return. The two of them had been allowed to attend a Guild event several months earlier, and Mom had told them not to touch any of the tasty treats floating past them on levitating trays.

"Oh, well I don't know about that," Mom said. "They'll probably have a separate table for children to eat at while the adults mingle."

"Can we explore?" Ryn asked.

"Probably not," Dad said.

"What if we're quiet?"

Dad raised an eyebrow. "When are the two of you ever quiet when you're playing?"

Ryn lifted his shoulders and gave his father a wide grin. "Never?"

"Exactly," Dad said, but Ryn could see he was trying to hide a smile.

A lurch in the region of Ryn's stomach told him the carriage had begun to descend. "Ooh, we're almost there!" He slid off the seat and pressed his face to the window. Reed joined him a second later, already pointing at something below.

"Boys, please." Mom leaned forward and tugged Ryn back onto the seat beside her, while Dad did the same with Reed on the other side of the carriage. "What did I say about keeping the windows clean? We need to return the carriage to the Guild in the same condition it was in when we picked it up."

"Don't worry, Mom," Reed said. "We didn't breathe on the glass. It's still clean."

As the carriage continued its descent, Mom gave them further instructions on how to behave themselves. It was all stuff Ryn had heard before, but clearly Mom thought he and Reed needed a reminder.

After they'd landed and climbed out of the carriage, they joined the other Guild members and their families on the paved pathway leading to the front door. Short lollipop-shaped trees lined the pathway on either side, decorated with tiny blue lights. Ryn held onto Mom's hand while trying to see past the other guests. It was nothing like his home, which was hidden inside a tree by glamour magic. This home was large and out in the open. He could see windows and balconies and vines creeping up the walls.

Just as Ryn was starting to get bored shuffling along the path, they reached the entrance. Mom and Dad greeted the hostess, and then he and Reed were introduced. They shook the woman's hand, smiled politely, and said, "Good evening, Councilor Valentia," just as they'd been taught. Finally, after moving beyond the front door, Mom allowed them to remove their jackets. As Ryn tugged his arms free, he looked around for Violet. Eventually he spotted her, clinging to her dad's side while he spoke with a bald man. She wore a pink dress with puffed sleeves and some kind of sparkly clip to hold her hair back, which was strange since she didn't normally wear dresses or put pretty things in her hair.

When Vi saw him and Reed, she smiled, waved, and ran toward them. "You guys missed the funniest thing." Her eyes sparkled with delight. "A lady had this long feather on her head, and it was so tall it touched one of the floating candles up there, and it caught alight! And then someone pushed her into the fountain!" She bounced up and down as she giggled. "Dad kept telling me to stop laughing, but I couldn't."

"Where did she go?" Reed asked, looking around as his smile grew.

"I don't know. Maybe one of the other rooms."

"What's outside?" Ryn asked. He tried to see between the guests to the other side of the room.

Vi shrugged. "Dad said I had to stay with him. But there were these two other kids here, and one was saying there are secret passages between the rooms upstairs."

"No way." Reed's eyes widened. "That's so cool."

"Maybe if there's three of us now, we can go play," Ryn said. "Ask your dad, Vi. And I'll ask Mom." He ran to Mom's side and tugged her hand, but she continued chatting and laughing with Councilor Valentia. He waited a few moments, then tugged again.

Finally, she looked down at him with a frown. "Ryn, I'm trying to have a conversation, and it's rude when you interrupt."

"I'm sorry." He tried to look suitably contrite. "But can we go play? Please?"

"I don't think so. I'm sure Councilor Valentia doesn't want you roaming around her house."

"Please, Mom," Reed said, joining Ryn. "I promise we'll be good."

"Oh, it's completely fine," Councilor Valentia said. "They can go wherever they want."

"Are you sure?"

"Yes, of course. Let them have fun." She beamed down at Reed. "Grown-up conversations are so boring, aren't they?"

He smiled back her and nodded. "Thank you, Councilor Valentia," he said politely.

The two of them ran back to Vi, Ryn feeling a twinge of irritation that Reed had once again so easily talked his way into getting something. But the feeling passed quickly. Ryn had never been able to stay mad at his brother for long.

"Garden or upstairs?" Reed asked.

Vi chewed her lip, then said, "I vote upstairs."

"Yeah," Ryn said. "Let's look for the secret passages."

They headed for the stairs, but Vi stopped a moment later. "Oh wow." She swung around. "Did you see that? The tray with the mini chocolate castles?"

"Yeah, those look amazing," Reed said, following her gaze.

Vi sighed. "I wish we could try them."

"We could," Ryn said, "if we just sneak some off the tray when no one's looking."

Vi's eyes widened. "What if we get in trouble?"

"And what about the secret passages?" Reed asked. "Secret passages are better than chocolate."

Vi pursed her lips, her brow creasing as she frowned. Ryn didn't think she agreed that secret passages were better than chocolate, but she shrugged and said, "Okay. Let's look for them."

Together they climbed the stairs, whispering about the treasures that might be hidden inside these secret passages.

"Maybe we should split up," Reed said when they reached the landing where an armchair, a bookcase, and a tall plant stood. One corridor led to the right and another to the left. "We'll have a better chance of finding the passages if we're searching in different places."

"Okay," Vi said, though her voice was hesitant. "Um, I'll go with you," she said to Reed.

Ryn was a little annoyed that he'd have to continue the search on his own, but he agreed that their odds of finding a secret passage were higher if they split up. "Okay. I'll go this way." He turned left and walked along the corridor, patting the walls as he went. He looked into the rooms that were open, searching for lines on the walls that might indicate a disguised door. But he found nothing exciting.

At the end of the corridor, a half-open door led to an extension of the party downstairs. It was a large room with a railing that looked over the hall below. Adults lounged in armchairs or stood in small groups, drinking colorful drinks and laughing, or leaning over the railing and waving politely at people below. Ryn was about to turn back when he saw a tray with tiny chocolate castles floating toward the other side of the room. He looked around, noting that no one was paying attention to him, then began walking. Not too quickly, as if he were running away from something, and not too slowly, as if he were trying to be sneaky. He simply walked.

When he reached the tray, he didn't look around. He knew he would appear guilty if he did that. He reached up with both hands, grabbed two chocolate castles, and walked back across the room without making eye contact with anyone.

When he'd returned to the safety of the corridor, he couldn't help laughing at his success. He put one castle in his mouth, then hurried back along the corridor as he chewed it. His hand was warm, and he didn't want the second chocolate to melt. He crossed the landing and entered the other corridor just as a voice spoke behind him.

"Ryn, where did you go?" Vi whispered loudly. He turned and found her at the top of the stairs. "I was looking for you. We found one. A door to a secret passage."

"Look what *I* found," Ryn said, holding out the chocolate delicacy.

"Ah, you got one!" she exclaimed, running over to him. "Did you get in trouble?"

He shook his head, smiling proudly. "Nope. No one saw me. Here, it's for you." He placed the castle on her outstretched palm.

"Wow. Thank you." She grinned at him, and he wasn't quite sure why he wanted to do what he was about to do, but it felt like the right moment. So he leaned forward and kissed her on the mouth. It was a quick kiss, and then he stepped back, looking at her startled expression. She blinked. Then she swished her skirt from side to side, smiled shyly, and said, "Thank you for the castle." With that, she turned and ran away.

CHAPTER 2

Present Day

RYN STOOD NEAR THE SEELIE COURT THRONE ROOM, remembering his first kiss and wondering at the odd similarities between that one and the kiss that had taken place several hours earlier today. Both had happened in or near a hidden passage, and both ended with Violet running away from him. At least she'd smiled the first time. This time ... Well, he'd thought it was pretty darn amazing. Vi, however, didn't seem to agree.

Movement on the stairs caught his attention, and he looked up to see her coming down. The dress the clothes caster had put her in this evening was purple and puffy. It didn't look too bad, but he'd bet anything she hated it. He tried to catch her gaze, but she didn't look his way. Was that intentional, or had she simply not seen him yet?

She headed straight for someone standing beside the throne room doors. A guy Ryn was certain she didn't know, despite the attention she was suddenly paying him. He debated whether to interrupt them and pull her aside so he could ask her what was wrong, but he didn't want to make a scene. She'd be even less likely to confide in him if he embarrassed her.

Dinner was worse. Though Vi sat right beside him, she didn't speak to him once, choosing instead to turn her body away and spend the entire evening in conversation with the guy on her other side. Ryn couldn't deny the jealousy that mingled with his confusion. He wanted so badly to talk to her, to demand an explanation for why she'd run off and was now pointedly ignoring him, but the single overwhelming emotion he felt rolling off her kept him quiet: fear. It made no sense. Why was she *afraid* of him? He needed to know, but now wasn't the time to ask. He would have to be patient and wait until he could get her alone after dinner.

That wasn't going to be as easy as he'd hoped, however. When dinner with the Seelie Queen was finished, Vi was the first one up and out of the room. Ryn pushed past the other graduates and hurried after her, determined to speak to her before she got away. "V, hang on," he called once he was out of the dining room. But instead of slowing, she walked faster, breaking into a run and disappearing around a corner. "Just wait, dammit." He began running. "Violet!" She stopped at the foot of the stairs, but didn't turn back. "I don't get it," he said, coming to a halt a few steps away from her. "What are you upset about?"

Slowly, she turned and faced him. He struggled to decipher the tumult of emotions that radiated from her. Fear was definitely still there, with fleeting moments of shame, desire, doubt. But Ryn's unique ability to sense the emotions of others was just as useless as ever at understanding the *reasons* for those emotions.

Eventually, Vi said, "Can we just pretend it didn't happen?"

Completely bewildered and more than a little hurt, Ryn couldn't think of what to say. Before he could figure out how to get an explanation out of her, she looked past him. Her eyes widened and her mouth dropped open. Ryn swung around, and there beneath an archway was the same man he and Vi had seen here last night. The man who looked exactly like Vi's father.

"Hey!" she shouted as the imposter turned and fled. "Stop!"

And once again, she was running away from him.

CHAPTER 3

THEY LEFT THE SEELIE PALACE THE FOLLOWING MORNING AND traveled home in silence, each lost in their own thoughts. If not for the massive revelation from the night before—the news that Vi's father was actually alive, that he'd been undercover all this time— Ryn would have pressed Vi for answers. Pleaded with her to explain herself. But he couldn't ask her now. What had happened between them was insignificant in comparison to the fact that *her father was alive*. Her thoughts must be consumed by this single fact, and Ryn didn't blame her. He could barely believe it himself.

He returned home and tried to distract himself, determined to give Vi the space she needed to come to terms with her father being alive. He waited all afternoon and most of the evening too, but eventually he couldn't stand it any longer. He had to speak to her. He needed to understand what she was afraid of.

He took the faerie paths to her home and waited outside for several moments. He should knock. That would be the polite thing to do. But if she saw it was him, she probably wouldn't let him inside. She probably wouldn't even open a doorway.

Good thing Ryn had been granted access to this home long ago and could let himself in. Once inside, he looked around, but couldn't find Vi in the living room or kitchen. He headed upstairs and crossed the landing to her bedroom. She was on the bed, looking at something on her amber. He leaned against the door frame and tapped his knuckles against it.

Her head whipped up, her body tensing at the sound. He waited for the fear he'd sensed at the graduation ball and again last night, but it was overshadowed by something far more pleasant. Something hot and heady that she stamped down a moment later. "You know you're supposed to stand *outside* and knock, right?" she said.

"Yes, but I figured you wouldn't let me in if you knew it was me. So I let myself in instead."

She leaned over and placed her amber on the bedside table, forcing out a laugh. "Why wouldn't I let you in?"

"Because you've been avoiding me since yesterday morning?" he suggested. "If I hadn't caught your father for you last night, you'd have hidden in your room all evening. And if we hadn't been forced to travel back together this morning, you definitely would have stayed away from me all day."

"Well, you know, we don't have to see each other every day."

That was true, but it was fast becoming obvious to Ryn that he *wanted* to see her every day. "I suppose not, but since there's this awkwardness between us, we should probably talk about it." He waited for her to respond, and when she didn't, he entered the room and moved toward the desk. "Why do I get the feeling our relationship is backwards?" He shrugged his jacket off and hung it over the back of the desk chair. "Isn't it usually the girl who always wants to talk about feelings and the guy who bottles everything up inside?"

"I don't bottle things up."

"Right. Of course not."

She pulled her knees up to her chest and wrapped her arms around them. Filigree, in the form of a white rabbit with wings, hopped to the edge of the bed and leaped off, flapping furiously as he attempted to fly toward Ryn. Ryn stretched his arms out and caught Filigree before he could fall.

"So, um, how's your mom going with that murder investigation?" Vi asked.

A not-so-subtle subject change. She really was planning to ignore the whole kiss thing. "Okay, since you clearly aren't going to be the one to bring it up," he said, "I'll say it. We kissed. It was pretty damn hot. Now I want to talk about it, but I can't because you're being all weird. That isn't normal for you. You're not like other girls, remember? You don't get silly and upset and moody. You're cooler than that."

"Well, Ryn, I guess I can only be cool up to a certain point. There's a line, and when you kissed me just to prove that you were right about something, you crossed it."

Ryn blinked. "Just to prove I was right?" Filigree struggled to free himself, so Ryn placed him on the floor. "What are you talking about?"

"You're going to tell me you don't remember?" Her eyebrows rose as she gave him a skeptical look. "Let me help you. We had the super-hot kiss, and then you ended it with, 'I told you that you were missing out.'"

"Yeah, so? You *were* missing out. I wasn't trying to prove a point; I was simply stating a fact. And that wasn't where I planned to end it." His skin heated at the memory of her legs wrapped around him, her lips pressing his, the sparks of magic darting across their skin. "Trust me, I could have stayed in the dark with you a whole lot longer if we hadn't hit the wrong wall and landed in the middle of a partially demolished sitting room. Speaking of which, you haven't asked me what happened after you bolted."

Feigning a bored tone, she asked, "What happened after I bolted?"

"Well, it turns out Mr. Faerie Sneak had just as much right to

16

be in there as we did. So we both agreed to pretend we'd never seen each other, and then he ran off while I was left to clean up all the mess you and I had made before Princess Olivia got back."

"*We* made?"

"Yes, V. Shattered vases, burning cushions, overturned furniture. That was us." He grinned. "It was one seriously hot kiss, remember?"

She didn't answer, but what she *felt* suggested she remembered the kiss the same way he did. She drew in a long breath. "Okay, fine," she said. "I'll talk. The kiss was hot. Amazing. Incredible. You were right—clearly I was missing out by never having experienced a kiss from someone magical. And now I know, so thank you. Can we move on?"

Never had anyone sent Ryn's heart on such a rollercoaster. One moment it seemed she'd enjoyed it as much as he had, and the next she wanted to move on. He crossed his arms. "I still don't get it. Why do you want to move on? It's not like you kissed me simply because you were bored and had nothing else to do at the time."

"Oh. Well, since you know so much about my motivations, maybe you'd like to tell me why I kissed you."

He threw his hands up, frustration finally getting the better of him. "Are you really not going to admit it?"

"Admit what?"

"You have feelings for me, Violet. Why is it so hard for you to say that?"

"Because it isn't true." Her arms tightened around her knees, and she refused to meet his gaze. "And because if it *were* true you'd only end up hurting me."

"That's ridiculous. If we have feelings for each other and we want to be together, why would I be stupid enough to hurt you?"

"Well, you probably wouldn't do it intentionally, but after a while you'd get over whatever feelings you might have for me." She glanced up, meeting his eyes for a moment, almost challenging him with her gaze. "I know you like the company of Undergrounders, and I can never be as exotic or exciting as the beings you'll find down there."

He walked forward, pressed both hands onto the bed, and leaned toward her. He made sure she was still looking at him as he said, "I don't *want* to be with any Undergrounder, V. *I want you.*"

He felt the effect of his words on her, and it gave him hope, but the thrill was quickly chased away by doubt. "You say that …"

"I *mean* that."

"You *think* you mean it, Ryn, and you probably do right now, but it won't last, and where will that leave me?"

"Violet. This … what I'm feeling …" He pushed away from the bed, struggling to find the right words. "It's so much more than anything I've ever felt for anyone. It's threatening to explode out of me. How can you tell me it won't last?"

"I don't know." She shrugged and shook her head. "I only know one thing for sure, and it's that you'll break my heart."

"No. I could never hurt you again, V. I *mean* it." He was becoming desperate now that he could sense her fear starting to blot everything else out again. "What do I have to say to make you believe me?"

"There isn't anything you can say, Ryn, or anything you can do. And it doesn't matter, anyway, because I don't feel that way about you. Things were good when we were friends. Why can't we just leave it at that?"

Ryn let out a laugh completely devoid of humor. "You don't feel that way about me? Now you're just lying."

"I am not."

"Yes, you are."

Her lips pressed together for a moment. Her hands tightened into fists. "You have no idea what I'm feeling, Oryn."

"I know exactly what you're—"

"You don't. End of conversation."

"YES I DO!" he shouted. "Aren't you listening to me? I *know* what you're feeling! I *feel* what you're feeling! You think you're the only one in Creepy Hollow graced with a dose of extra special magic? Well, you're not. I feel every single flipping thing everyone around me is feeling, which, when it comes to you, usually isn't much. But guess what? That isn't the case anymore. I knew you were panicking when we headed onto the dance floor after graduation because I *felt* it. I knew that the moment I whispered in your ear while we were dancing was the moment you realized just how much you wanted me because I *felt* the flood of emotions that suddenly came over you. I felt it again yesterday morning when I was lying next to you in bed, and again when I was kissing you. I *know*, Violet, so don't lie to me."

Shocked silence greeted his outburst, and Ryn immediately regretted his honesty. He hadn't meant to say any of that. He hadn't meant to tell her about this odd magical ability he possessed. Not tonight, anyway. He wanted her to trust him, to feel safe, before she discovered that he could feel everything she felt.

Finally, she whispered, "What ... what am I feeling now?"

Anyone who'd been watching this exchange could have accurately guessed most of what Vi was feeling, so it wasn't as if this would prove anything. But he may as well say it out loud. "Up until about a minute ago, it was mostly desire and fear mixed in together, but right now, shock is pretty much overshadowing everything else."

The way she looked at him now ... it was as if he were a stranger. "How long have you known you can do this?"

"A long time," he admitted quietly.

"And you never told me."

"I—"

"You've always known my secret, and yet you never bothered to tell me yours."

Dammit, this was all going wrong. He struggled to separate her intense anger from his own emotions. "Violet, I—"

"Get out of my house."

Not working. He didn't know if it was her anger or his that slammed into him, but his patience was suddenly at its end. He grabbed his jacket from the back of the chair and headed for the door. "Gladly. If you want to keep lying to yourself, go right ahead."

CHAPTER 4

"THANKS FOR THE DEMONSTRATION," RYN SAID, DUCKING HIS head as the carpet he was sitting on zoomed in through the shop door and glided to a halt on the floor. He and the green-haired shopkeeper stood up and walked off the carpet, which promptly rolled itself up and moved to a corner of the shop.

"As you can see," the shopkeeper said, his words accented to the point where Ryn could barely understand him, "the carpet made no attempt to throw us off at any stage. A recent breakthrough in carpet-flying magic."

Ryn nodded. "And it seems fairly easy to steer."

"Very easy. So you are happy with it?"

"Yes, this is exactly what I'm looking for." Ryn leaned on the counter and signed the agreement the shopkeeper had drawn up for him before taking him on a test ride. "So you'll meet me there just after sunset tonight with the carpet?"

"Yes. I know how to get there now."

"Great. Thanks very much." He shook the man's hand and strode out of the store. Once outside, he opened a faerie paths doorway on the nearest wall. He was already late for his next meeting—with the specialist who'd installed the glow-bug lighting system throughout the Guild—and he didn't want to keep the woman waiting any longer.

Half an hour later, after Ryn had explained exactly what he wanted and Marlia, the glow-bug specialist, had written and altered and rewritten a spell for him, Ryn allowed himself to start getting excited about his plan.

"That should do it," Marlia said, rolling up the paper and handing it to Ryn.

"And it'll work even if I'm not right next to the bugs? If they can't physically hear me?"

"Yes, but it will obviously take longer for the call to reach the ones that are farther away."

Ryn nodded. "Got it."

"So." She sat back in her chair, tucking her sleek white hair behind one pointed ear. "Are you going to tell me why you want all the glow-bugs in the whole of Creepy Hollow forest to fly into the sky at the same time?"

Ryn smiled, remembering what Vi had said the night they'd discussed impressive stunts. *Jeez, I don't know, Ryn. Like a gazillion glow-bugs lighting up the night sky with their tiny glowing butts or something.* He'd laughed then, but he hadn't forgotten her words. If that's what it took to make her realize how serious he was about his feelings for her, he would do it. "Call it an impressive stunt," he told Marlia. "To prove myself to someone."

She raised an eyebrow and muttered, "Young people."

CHAPTER 5

RYN STOOD OUTSIDE THE TREE THAT CONCEALED VI'S HOME, unaccustomed to the nerves chewing at his insides. If this didn't work—if he couldn't convince her how much she really meant to him—it might actually break his heart. It wasn't a position he'd ever found himself in before. It was silly next to the high-stakes matters he often ended up involved in as a guardian. It was silly next to all the information Vi's dad had piled on top of him and Vi the other night. It didn't *feel* silly, though. Right now, it felt like it mattered more than anything else in the world.

So he took a deep breath and knocked against the tree, bracing himself for the flood of anger that might soon be coming his way. Then he held Vi's gift behind his back. It wasn't long before a portion of the tree rippled and vanished, revealing Vi standing in the doorway. Her hopeful expression fell the moment she saw him, but instead of disappointment or anger, he sensed something else.

"My, uh, long-lost relative isn't here tonight," she said, cryptically referring to her father, "so unless you're here to visit Filigree, there isn't anyone in this home who wants to see you."

If that were true, she would have closed the door already. But she was still standing there. Standing there and feeling … "Why are you nervous?" he asked.

She placed her hands on her hips. "Is there no way you can turn that off? Because I really don't appreciate you knowing exactly what I'm feeling."

"Nope. Trust me, if there was a way to turn it off, I would have found it by now."

Her gaze brushed over him. "Are you going to tell me why you're here?"

"Are you going to invite me in?" Instead of answering, she simply stood there. She still hadn't closed the door, though, which kicked his confidence up a notch. "Fine," he said eventually. "It's your birthday tomorrow. I'd like to give you something."

"You already gave me something. New amber and an expensive charm."

"Okay, well, now I have something else to give you." He smiled, attempting to lighten the mood. "And it's rude to refuse a gift."

She raised an eyebrow. "And yet we both know being rude has never been a problem when it comes to the two of us."

Darn this silly girl and her stubbornness. She sure wasn't going to make this easy. Ryn studied his feet for a moment before locking his eyes on her once more. "Please?" As she hesitated, he tried to read her emotions, but it was becoming difficult to tell the difference between the ones that belonged to her and the ones that belonged to him. He wasn't sure if the heat curling inside his stomach was his reaction to her, or the other way around. Hopefully both.

She cleared her throat. "Um, okay, come in."

"Actually, I don't want to give it to you here. I'd like you to come somewhere with me."

"Is this something to do with the party Tora and Raven are planning? Because I thought that was tomorrow."

"It is tomorrow. And since you don't like surprises, I'll tell you exactly what time it is and who's coming if you'll just follow me now."

"You're being weird."

"And I'll be even weirder and get down on my knees and beg, if I have to. I've done it before, remember?" And he would do it again in a heartbeat if it would help him now.

"Okay, okay, I'll go with you. Just let me get my boots."

"And a jacket," he added. "You might get cold."

She disappeared into the house and returned moments later. "Where are we going?" she asked as she sealed the entrance to her home.

"You'll see." He opened a doorway in the air and reached for her hand, grateful for the excuse to hold it. As darkness enveloped them, the memory of their kiss in the secret passageway came to mind. Heat crawled up his neck and toward his face. He longed to pull her closer and find her lips with his, but—*Focus.* He blinked against the darkness and pointed his thoughts firmly toward the old gargan tree. As light appeared around them, Vi dropped his hand. She walked ahead of him across one of the enormous ancient branches. Beyond her, the setting sun lit up the evening sky with a thousand dazzling shades of orange and red. Ryn couldn't have created anything more perfect if he'd been able to paint the sky himself.

Violet tilted her head up and gazed at the sky, a smile parting her lips. "Do you remember that poem by Mil Crowthorn about the riches of nature?"

He did. His mother and Vi's mother had collected poetry books the way other people collected coins or cards. As children, he and Vi had read through them, marking their favorites and memorizing verses for school. Then they'd parted ways, and Ryn had pretended he had little interest in something as silly as poetry, never telling anyone about the words he would occasionally scribble down in his attempt to rid himself of the tide of emotions that sometimes assaulted him from all sides.

"'Give me the setting sun," he quoted, "'and I'll be a richer man than most / For never have I seen gold like that which glows above the earth. / Give me the night sky, and I'll be rich beyond all ruin / For never have I seen diamonds like those that dance beside the moon.'"

He stopped himself before he could recite any more of the poem. It hadn't been part of the plan, this cheesy, poetry-quoting moment. He fully expected Vi to roll her eyes, maybe even smack him over the head. But instead she nodded, her eyes still glued to the sunset. "Yes. That's how I feel. I don't need anything more for my birthday than that sky."

Ryn stepped closer and held his gift out to her. "Maybe just this."

Hesitantly, she took it. She removed the silver string, and the silk layers fell away, revealing the colorful ribbons she'd found in her mother's hiding place at the Seelie Court. Ribbons that were now fashioned into a simple bracelet, held together on either end with a silver bead. Ryn held his breath, hoping she wouldn't hate what he'd asked Raven to do. Hoping Vi wouldn't think the ribbons were now ruined. Her emotions seemed to say otherwise, but for some reason, she wasn't saying anything. "The ribbons looked so pretty on your arm," he said, feeling the need to explain himself, "so I took them to Raven and asked her to make them into a bracelet." He took it from her and tied it around her wrist.

"I should probably be creeped out that you snuck into my house and stole the ribbons," she said quietly, "but it's so beautiful that I'll forgive you for your sneaking."

"So you like it?" he asked, needing confirmation, not fully trusting her feelings.

She looked up at him and smiled. "I love it."

He smiled in response and almost gave in to the urge to kiss her right then and there, but his amber shivered in his pocket. He would have ignored it if he hadn't been expecting to hear from the owner of the carpet store. He pulled his amber out and looked at the words on the surface, glad to see a message from the shopkeeper. "If you don't mind," he said to Vi as he put the amber away, "I'd like to take you somewhere else now."

"Um, okay. But this had better not be a ploy to get me to go on a date with you."

"Not at all." Before stepping away, he leaned closer and whispered, "It's so much better than that."

He walked past her to where the shopkeeper had just appeared with the rolled-up carpet tucked beneath his arm. "Am I late?" he asked quietly after Ryn greeted him.

"No. Perfect timing, actually." Ryn took the carpet. "I'll return it before midnight." The shopkeeper turned away, and Ryn walked back to Vi's side. "Here we go." He placed the carpet on the branch at their feet, grabbed one end, flicked it open—and watched it float into the air.

Vi took a step back. "What—what is that?"

"Exactly what it looks like: a magic carpet."

"But ... magic carpets don't exist."

"And yet," Ryn said, loving how surprised she was, "there's one floating right here in front of you. How strange is that?" He stepped onto it, turned to face her, and held is hand out.

She eyed the carpet warily. "I ... don't know if I trust that thing."

"It's perfectly safe. I've done some reading on the subject. Turns out there have been some major advances in carpet flying magic in the past few years." He grinned. "They no longer throw people off." Her eyes widened, which probably wasn't a good sign. "And guess what?" he added quickly. "You're a faerie, which means if this carpet *does* decide to throw you off, you can easily slow your fall with magic."

"I … okay." She reached for his hand and let him pull her up. Then she crouched down, using her arms to balance herself, while Ryn sat cross-legged and reached back for the two corners of the carpet behind him. Slowly, the carpet began to rise. Ryn steered between the branches as the carpet soared higher, slowly gaining speed. He pulled the edge of the carpet higher up behind him, testing the acceleration. With a sudden burst of speed, the carpet shot out above the highest branches, revealing the entirety of the Creepy Hollow forest spread out below them. Vi leaned to one side, staring down with wide eyes and parted lips.

"Kind of amazing, isn't it?" Ryn said. The carpet slowed as he released the corners. He climbed carefully to his feet. "You should stand up. It's more exciting." He held his hand out again. "I know how you like a thrill." After a moment's pause, she placed her hand in his and let him pull her up. As the carpet rippled gently beneath their feet, they stood together and watched the sun dip below the horizon. Ryn stole the occasional glance at her, watching the breeze lift her hair, watching her smile in awe. He was eager to get to the last part of his plan, but he needed it to be darker first. As stars slowly began to appear across the sky, they didn't speak. He didn't sense any awkwardness, though. It was enough to simply appreciate one another's company and the beauty of their surroundings.

Eventually, when Ryn determined it was dark enough, he said, "I have one more surprise for you." He moved behind Violet and covered her eyes with his hands. She flinched—he probably should have warned her—but didn't protest. With nervous anticipation coming to life inside him, he began chanting the call spell Marlia had given him. He spoke carefully, not wanting to get a single word wrong, repeating the chant as he'd been instructed. It soon felt as if the words were being pulled from his tongue, streaming forward and being carried away on an enchanted breeze to find every glow-bug in the forest.

The first ones appeared quickly, flitting up from the tops of the trees and hanging in the air all around them. As he continued the chant, more and more glow-bugs appeared, until a bright golden glow surrounded the carpet. By the time he finished speaking, Vi was leaning back against his chest, more relaxed than he'd sensed in ages. He tilted his head down, closer to her ear, and whispered so he wouldn't startle her. "You said there was nothing I could say or do to convince you that my feelings for you are real and long-lasting. Well, clearly I took that as a challenge, and since it'll apparently take the shining butts of a gazillion glow-bugs to prove myself to you, here they are." He pulled his hands away and watched as she opened her eyes.

He couldn't describe the emotion that shot through her body in that moment, but it sent a shiver racing through him and raised the hairs on his arms. As her wide-eyed gaze moved across the sky, something told him he'd succeeded in amazing her. But then, as if to prove him wrong, her emotions began to shift. Hesitation, doubt. Fear again.

"This is incredible, Ryn. It is. But—"

"No." He took her arm and carefully turned her to face him. "No buts. You think I'm going to hurt you? You think I'm going to get bored and run off with some Undergrounder the first chance I get? You obviously have no idea how *amazing* you are. You, Violet Fairdale, are incredible, and I want you. *Every part of you.*" His heart pounded painfully in his chest as he realized this was it. His last chance to make her see that he meant every single thing he was saying. If she didn't believe him here, in this moment, she probably never would. "I want your stubbornness and your sarcasm and your competitive spirit. I want you challenging me and fighting beside me. I want to hold you and kiss you and *so much more* because there's no one else in the world who knows me like you do." The words were tumbling out of him now, too quickly for him to pause and consider the most eloquent way to impart everything he felt for her. "You have always been the one for me, even when we couldn't stand each other. You're beautiful and hot and sexy all at once, *and* you're more intelligent than any girl I've ever met. I love the fact that I've known you all my life. It just feels *right* when you're beside me. It feels like I've been lost in the desert for years, and ... I've finally come home."

There it was. Everything he felt, his whole heart, laid out in front of her. She couldn't possibly have any doubt now about the way he felt. And yet ... there it was again. That fear that always crept back in and smothered everything else she was feeling.

Ryn grabbed her shoulders and shook them, because dammit, if something was going to keep them apart, it would have to be a real obstacle, not this ridiculous certainty she had that he would somehow hurt her. "Stop being so scared, V! You're one of the bravest people I know. Why can't you let go of this fear?"

Her lips parted, but no words came out. She seemed to be looking beyond him, lost in her own thoughts, and her emotions were shifting in a way he couldn't figure out.

"Please say something, V."

Still she didn't speak, but she was feeling ... feeling ... he couldn't be sure, and he didn't dare to hope because what if he was wrong? What if she was about to refuse him forever?

"Violet, please. Say something. I swear, you're going to break my heart if you don't—"

She kissed him. Her body was suddenly against his, her arms around his neck, and surprise and joy and desire collided into him all at once. In the heady rush of the moment, he lost his balance. The two of them tumbled onto the carpet, and then Vi was straddling his waist, her lips grazing his neck as he traced his hands up her back and into her hair. He pulled her face closer, meeting her lips with his. Magic heated his skin, and sparks danced across their bodies, and he didn't think he'd ever been happier.

He didn't need her to answer in words. This was answer enough.

DATE NIGHT

This story takes place several months after *The Faerie War*.
I asked readers what bonus Creepy Hollow content they'd like to
read, and the overwhelming response boiled down to the following:
pretty much anything featuring Violet and Ryn,
with a bit of adventure and romance.

The result of that was … *Date Night*.

Read this story any time after *The Faerie War*,
Creepy Hollow Book Three.

CHAPTER 1

"AND ... DONE." RYN LARKENWOOD SNAPPED THE ENCHANTED handcuffs in place onto the elf's wrists and looked around the casino's private gaming room for his partner Berian. The room was empty aside from several upturned chairs, a large, cracked poker table, and dozens of playing cards and chips scattered across the carpeted floor. No Berian. Pretentious asshat still hadn't arrived. "Typical," Ryn muttered.

He and Berian had been tracking Elis Dei's activities for the past two weeks. Well, Ryn had been doing a lot of tracking; Berian had been pretending to keep up. It seemed the elf had been using various enchantments to conceal his location, so Vi's ability to find people—which the Guild still knew nothing about—wasn't much help, and Ryn had had to go old school with his methods.

But the enchantments must have begun to wear off, because earlier that afternoon, Vi had hurried into Ryn's cubicle at the new Guild and whispered that she'd seen Dei in a casino inside one of the fae realm's most opulent hotels. After reporting it as an anonymous tip, Ryn had raced off to apprehend Dei. Berian was supposed to meet him at the casino to assist with the arrest, but he had never shown.

35

So Ryn had had no choice but to go in on his own. Elis Dei had been 'disguised' in oversized rose-tinted glasses and a wig of scruffy dark hair long enough to hide his pointed ears, but Ryn knew his face well enough by now to recognize him. The scuffle had been brief—Ryn had barely broken a sweat—and the other players had scattered the moment they realized a guardian was in the room. In under a minute, the drug-potion dealing elf was in cuffs.

Berian would not be pleased. *Wait for me there*, his last scribbled amber message had said. *Don't return to the Guild without me.* Ryn figured he probably wanted to ensure he also got credit for this arrest. Berian was originally from some tiny Guild hardly anyone had ever heard of and had graduated top of his class. Arrogant, rude, and not nearly as remorseful as he should be for unintentionally fighting on the wrong side after The Destruction, he annoyed the heck out of Ryn. Ryn certainly wasn't about to wait for him now that the job was done. He had a date to get to.

Slot machine tunes and the happy ringing of a jackpot enchantment reached Ryn's ears from the casino's main floor. Stale smoke irritated the back of his throat, and a thousand different emotions assaulted his mind. He blocked them out as best he could, though he couldn't quite ignore the ache in his chest brought on by an overwhelm of feelings that weren't his own.

Dei struggled against him, as if he thought there was some chance he might actually be able to escape Ryn and make a run for it. "You know what makes me sick?" Ryn said, pushing the elf toward the door. "We saved the world for *everyone*. That includes you. And what did you turn around and do the second Draven's reign ended? You decided to take advantage of the very people who gave up everything to ensure you could have a free life. Oh, and now you're gambling away your criminal fortune, because *that* makes so much sense."

"You know what makes *me* sick?" Dei growled. "Some prepubescent faerie waltzing in here thinking he can bring down my entire empire."

Ryn tightened his grip on Dei, his decidedly *non*-prepubescent arm muscles growing taut. "First of all, if I was waltzing, you'd know about it. I happen to be an excellent dancer. Secondly, the part that should make you feel sick is the thought of all the lives you've ruined with your illegal mind-numbing potions."

"Not my fault if lives have been ruined. I've never forced anything on anyone. People know exactly what they're buying when they come to me."

"You really do make me sick," Ryn muttered in disgust, frog-marching the elf across the casino floor. Since faerie paths couldn't be opened from within the casino—all magic-use was blocked, for obvious reasons, guardian weapons being the only exception—Ryn first had to navigate the maze of enchanted machines, endless flashing lights, tables, waitstaff, patrons, and, *finally*, security.

Stopping in the glittering, marble-floored atrium just outside the casino, Ryn released one of Dei's arms and reached inside his jacket for his amber. A quick glance told him there were no new messages from Berian. But there was something from Vi.

Rain check. AGAIN. So sorry. Have to hang out at a stuffy art gallery tonight instead :(

Ryn sighed as he slipped the amber back into his pocket and pulled out his stylus. How hard was it to go on a simple date? Admittedly, the dates he planned were never actually of the *simple* variety, but that wasn't the reason none of them had taken place yet. Something always came up. A drunk faerie accidentally setting himself on fire in the middle of a human high school prom. A river running down the main staircase of the new Guild. A swarm of enchanted books chasing children out of a school library. There were just as many everyday magical mishaps—alongside more serious law-breaking activities, of course—as there had been before The Destruction, but these days there were fewer guardians to deal with them.

"Time to go," Ryn said, directing Dei toward the nearest wall.

"So soon?" Dei asked, twisting out of Ryn's one-handed grip and whipping around to face him. Ryn waited to see if he would attempt to run, but it seemed the elf possessed some intelligence after all. Instead of answering, Ryn stepped past him and raised his stylus to the wall. Dei could try to get away if he wanted to, but the cuffs wouldn't allow him to use magic. It would take mere seconds for Ryn to catch him.

"What's the rush?" Dei asked, the first hint of uneasiness evident in his tone. "Got somewhere better to be?"

"Actually, yes. With the love of my life."

"Right, of course." Dei let out a grunt that was possibly meant to be a laugh. "It's Friday night date night and there's some desperate female waiting around for you to try to get into her—"

Quick as a flash, Ryn had the elf shoved against the wall, his forearm crushing Dei's throat and a glittering knife pressed to the base of his throat. "Finish that sentence," Ryn challenged in a voice deadly quiet, his tone suggesting the words would be the last Dei ever spoke, should he decide to finish the sentence after all.

"You can't ... kill me," Dei managed to say, his words a raspy whisper. "That's ... against ... the rules."

"True. But you don't need your tongue, do you? I doubt anyone would miss it."

Dei stared back at him, gritting his teeth, a challenge in his steely eyes. But he said nothing. Ryn released the knife and switched his stylus back to his right hand. With one arm still pressed to Dei's throat, he swiftly wrote a doorway spell on the wall. "Move," he said, directing the elf sideways as the dark, silent relief of the paths beckoned.

CHAPTER 2

Violet Fairdale glided across the interior room of the art gallery in a black figure-hugging dress that was both jaw-droppingly stunning and horrendously uncomfortable. The fabric stretched across her chest, looped around her neck, and ran down the length of her right arm, forming a skin-tight sleeve all the way to her wrist. Her left arm was entirely bare.

She didn't particularly enjoy the feeling of being strangled by her own outfit. She wasn't wild about its asymmetry either. What was the point of having *one* sleeve? But there was no use dwelling on her discomfort, or her inability to breathe properly while sucking her stomach in so tightly. She had accepted the assignment —and the dress—without complaint, and the sooner she got this over with, the sooner she could get on with her evening. Or, more accurately, the sooner she and Ryn could get on with *their* evening.

Vi's eyes trailed over the framed paintings on the walls, each piece displayed beneath its own spotlight. Despite what she'd told Ryn, the gallery and its black-tie fundraiser event were anything but stuffy. The high ceilings and generous spacing between artworks gave the area a decidedly open feel. At the very center of the room sat an impressive glass sculpture of a woman emerging from a wave, her arms spread wide and her head tilted upward. Men in tuxedos and women in glamorous gowns traveled the room, admiring the artwork and discussing potential bids.

With considerable effort, Vi resisted the urge to tug the constricting fabric away from her throat as she circled the sculpture, her eyes still on the walls. She couldn't help thinking that if Raven had crafted this dress, instead of whoever the Guild currently had working in their costume department, it would have been both magnificent *and* comfortable. And it wouldn't have been so tight around her legs. What if things got exciting and she had to actually fight someone? She couldn't even say she was surprised. Everyone at the Guild was so overworked these days that it was easy to overlook small but important details like—

Ah. There it was. Vi stopped as her gaze landed on the painting depicting a smudgy nighttime scene with a scattering of stars that seemed, by some trick of the light, to twinkle. Except, as Vi was aware after having spoken to the gallery director, it was no trick of the light. This painting originated in the fae realm, and the materials used to create it contained traces of magic. The enchantment was subtle—she might have missed it if she didn't know this was the painting she was looking for—so it was a good thing she'd spoken to the director.

That was the only reason she'd been required to dress up and allow herself to be visible for this last-minute assignment. She'd cornered the director, given him what she hoped was a conspiratorial smile, and asked about the 'special, otherworldly' item that her imaginary client had heard about. After a moment's pause, the director had matched her smile, dipped his head, and described the painting. Then, with a slight frown, he'd added, "I thought I knew all the interested parties who are aware of the painting's true origin, but I don't think I've met you before." His eyes traveled down her bare arm, landing on the guardian markings on her wrist, which she hadn't bothered to hide. The markings generally didn't mean anything to humans. "You are …"

"Hungry," Vi had told him, well aware that he was asking for her name and deciding he didn't need to know it. "I'm going to find some of those tasty-looking little appetizers I walked past a minute ago. Thank you for your help. I'm so looking forward to the auction."

Okay, time to disappear, Vi told herself, pulling her eyes from the painting and looking around for the nearest exit. Her plan was to re-enter the room with her glamour back in place, create a distraction with a little magic, and quietly remove the painting from the wall while everyone's attention was pointed elsewhere. Then she would head straight back to the Guild via the faerie paths, and this long day would finally be over.

She'd already prevented three magical incidents in the human realm today. She'd been all set to leave the Guild and relax for an hour or two before meeting Ryn when she'd been handed an assignment scroll and a black dress and told there was no one else currently available to deal with this vision. The details from the Seer had been sparse: *Bronze Edge Art Gallery. Auction event. Stolen magical painting. Can't see what it looks like. The gallery director knows. Find out from him which one it is. Retrieve it before the auction. Don't let the man with the blue bow tie touch it. Shattered glass. Injured people.*

That was it.

Well, Mr. Blue Bow Tie, whoever he was, wouldn't be getting anywhere near this painting now that Vi had identified it. She turned, ready to glide her way back across the room—thanks to the anti-trip charm she'd applied to her heels earlier—and almost bumped into someone.

"Berian," she said in surprise. She blinked, her thoughts stalling for a second. Then her heart squeezed and her breath caught. "What happened? Is Ryn okay?" Because that was surely the only reason Ryn's partner would show up at one of her assignments out of the blue.

Blue.

Her gaze flicked down, and there it was: a blue bow tie. Sitting snugly against the hollow of Berian's throat.

Crap.

"Probably not," Berian said, and Vi barely had a moment to register that he was answering her question before he shoved her backward. Darkness seeped into her vision on both sides, and she realized she'd been pushed through a faerie paths doorway—straight into someone else's grip. With zero hesitation, she brought her heel down hard and jerked her head backward. She connected with something—

—a cry of pain—

—the grip loosened—

—the doorway was closing—

—Berian's slimy smile—

Magic erupted from Vi's fingertips as she ripped free of her assailant's hold and launched forward, back into the human realm and straight at Berian. She caught a glimpse of his startled expression before crashing into him. They were on the floor, a snarl on his lips, his body angling to thrust her away just as the heel of her palm slammed into his chin.

His head snapped back. Fiery sparks burned in his palms. Someone screamed.

Vi threw herself off Berian, ducking her head as he hurled magic in her direction. It sizzled past her in a flash. Part of her brain was yelling at her that all of this was *visible* to a room full of humans—which would mean a giant clean-up operation of memory spells later tonight—while another part registered that Berian's magic was streaking straight toward the glass sculpture.

It struck.

Vi's hands flew up instinctively as she threw shield magic

around the exploding mass of glass shards. They struck her invisible layer of magic before raining down onto the gallery floor. Vi's attention snapped back to Berian as she rose swiftly to her feet—

Too late. He was already up. He barreled into her, knocking the air from her lungs and sending the two of them hurtling into the darkness of the faerie paths.

CHAPTER 3

DRAVEN'S WINTER WAS GONE, BUT AN ICY BREEZE HERALDED the imminent arrival of genuine winter as Ryn and his captive stepped out of the faerie paths into Creepy Hollow. Branches quivered and swayed, and moonlight danced in streaks across the forest floor. A pair of glimmering eyes peered at Ryn from the shadows.

The Guild's hidden entrance lay a few paces away. Ryn pushed Elis Dei ahead of him, but the elf had barely taken a step when the air rippled on the other side of the Guild entrance. Ryn pulled Dei to a halt as a doorway opened and out strode …

Berian. Plus a second guardian, both of them clutching … a black-clad body?

"Oh, great, I'm not too late," Berian said, stopping a few feet away. "I was hoping I'd catch you before you got inside."

Ryn narrowed his eyes, immediately suspicious. Berian was supposed to be meeting him at a casino right now, not showing up in the middle of Creepy Hollow in the company of another guardian—Cyrilla? She was also new, but Ryn was fairly sure that was the tall blond guardian's name—with a motionless body draped between them.

"What took you so damn long?" Dei demanded, tugging

44

against Ryn's hold. "And why didn't you warn me this idiot was on his way?" He jerked his head backward at Ryn.

What the … Ryn's blood chilled as the implication of Dei's words settled into his mind.

"I knew I wouldn't get there in time," Berian said. "Had to make a quick detour and grab some insurance." He shifted the body and let it slump to the ground.

And that was when time stopped for Ryn.

Purple hair. Guardian markings identical to his own. A face that filled his dreams at night. A slight body as still as stone.

Utterly … horrifyingly … still.

A distant roar filled Ryn's ears, and a shot of pure terror chilled the very core of his being.

Then everything raced back into motion and the sounds of the forest flooded his ears. He brought his elbow down hard, slamming Dei to the ground. With one boot pressed solidly onto his back and a glittering arrow aimed straight at the elf's head, he raised his hard gaze to Berian. "What did you do?" His quiet voice was as icy as the wind that shook the branches.

"Relax. She's not dead. Just stunned."

Warmth stole through Ryn's frozen body. His world, which for several paralyzing moments had teetered on the brink of a dark chasm, righted itself. He narrowed his eyes further as something hot and bitter burned through him, taking the place of his relief. "You're working with *him*?" he demanded, grinding his boot a little harder into Dei's back.

"I am."

Ryn shook his head in disgust. Now it made sense that Berian, supposedly an excellent guardian, had been so useless at tracking Elis Dei. No doubt he'd been doing his best to keep Ryn *away* from the drug-dealing elf these past two weeks. "So the guardian oath you took means nothing to you."

"You don't know a thing about me, Ryn."

"Clearly. You'd rather—"

"Okay, look," Berian interrupted. "This is simple. Hand over Dei, and in exchange you get Violet. Then we can all be on our merry way. We'll find some other part of the world in which to continue making our fortune, and you and your high school sweetheart can grow old together in Creepy Hollow."

Ryn got the feeling—quite literally—that Berian was making fun of him. Which was especially annoying considering that growing old with Vi right here in Creepy Hollow was exactly what he hoped to do. They were currently both still living in the Fireglass Vale base, along with dozens of other guardians and their families, but that wouldn't last forever. Soon enough, they'd be back in Creepy Hollow where they belonged.

"Fine," Ryn said. He had no intention of letting Berian and Dei get away, but he would make sure Vi was safe first before tracking them down again. He let go of the bow and arrow, and they disappeared. With a quick zap of magic, the enchanted cuffs were gone from Dei's wrists. Before the elf could stand, Ryn stepped over him and moved to Vi's side. He had her in his arms and with a shield up in front of them before Dei was on his feet.

"Great," Berian said. "Time for us to get out of here."

"You're not going to get rid of them?" Dei asked, rolling his shoulders and brushing dirt off his suit jacket as he strode toward Berian.

"I'm not *that* terrible," Berian said, looking somewhat affronted.

With a *how-stupid-are-you* look, Dei said, "Well I am. And so is she." He pointed past Ryn, and Ryn had less than a second in which to realize that Cyrilla was nowhere in sight.

He ducked. Stunner magic flew past his ear and struck his shield, which fortunately survived the hit. He placed Vi on the ground—well, more like dropped, but he could apologize for that later if they got out of here alive—and spun around, hands raised, magic streaking away from him. Silently, he cursed his lack of attention to detail. Cyrilla must have slipped away and circled around him while he'd been focused on Vi. He couldn't remember seeing her since the moment she and Berian had lowered Vi's body to the ground, and now she was hurling bullet-sized stones and guardian knives and a whirlwind of sand at him.

He deflected them all with a powerful blast of air before letting his own blade spin toward her. She danced aside, and he sensed his shield vanish as more magic struck it from somewhere behind him. *Thanks a lot, Berian.* He whipped back around to make sure nothing struck Vi—

But she was already up. "Got it," she gasped, slicing a sword through the air to knock an arrow off its course before throwing her own shield of magic between her and Berian and Dei.

"Welcome back," Ryn said, a grin on his lips as he turned just in time to deflect an arrow from Cyrilla. Then, abandoning weapons and magic, Cyrilla ran at him.

He was on the ground, the scent of damp earth filling his nostrils and a fist swinging toward his face. He grabbed the fist and twisted, then shoved her body clear of his. She rolled out of his reach and leaped up, just as he did the same.

"Not sure I can … hold this … much longer," Vi panted from behind him, presumably referring to her shield magic. "I'm still a little … out of it. And *crap* it's cold out here."

"Open a doorway," Ryn told her, ducking a kick from Cyrilla before landing his own kick to her stomach. She staggered backward with a grunt.

"Done," Vi answered.

Ryn spun around and grabbed her hand, and together they raced across the doorway's threshold—just as a bright flash of magic obliterated Vi's shield. Something crashed into Ryn's back, and then another something shoved him to the side. Still clasping Vi's hand tightly, he did his best to tear free of the claw-like grip on his shoulder as darkness enveloped them completely.

"Got you," a feminine voice hissed in his ear, and even though he knew it was Cyrilla and not some creepy ghost creature conjured from the infinite depths of the faerie paths, Ryn couldn't help the chill that skittered up the back of his neck.

Faint light seeped through the darkness, and he and Vi landed in a heap of limbs and leaves and sparks of magic. They were somewhere else in the forest—a clearing illuminated by clusters of glow-bugs—and Cyrilla and Berian had come through with them. A quick glance around the area revealed vases of flowers, small statues, and other trinkets balanced on fallen logs and giant tree roots.

And people. Fae. Three of them, as far as Ryn could tell. At the sudden appearance of the newcomers in their midst, one of them screamed. Two grasped hands, and then all three of them ran into the darkness, hopefully to find a safer spot to open a doorway to the paths.

Good, Ryn thought as he kicked Berian away from him. *Keep going. Get far away from here.* He rose quickly to his feet. Vi was already up, her bow raised, an arrow streaking toward Cyrilla as the latter rolled hastily out of the way. Ryn turned his back to Vi's, reached into the air, and gripped a blade in each hand as his narrowed gaze fell on Berian.

Then the air was filled with the sound of something ripping, and Berian was racing at him with a guttural cry, and after that the scene became a blur of dazzling magic, glittering weapons, fists and elbows and boots. It wasn't the ideal date night, but there was a significant part of Ryn that was actually enjoying it— and he knew he wasn't alone. He didn't have to feel the adrenaline high racing through Vi's body to be fully aware that she was having fun too. Dodge, spin, kick, duck—

Everything was … sideways?

He was on the ground.

Blinking.

A ringing sound in his ears.

The blurry glimmer of a guardian weapon growing smaller and smaller.

He pushed himself up as fast as his spinning head would allow. The ringing disappeared, making way for the sounds of rustling leaves and hurried footsteps and Berian saying, "Quickly! While they're both down!" Ryn blinked away enough of his dizziness to see Berian dragging Cyrilla from the clearing and into the surrounding shadows.

"Don't be a fool!" she protested, tugging free of his hold. "We have to get rid of them!"

Ryn raised his arms, a bow and arrow materializing in his—

Thwip.

An arrow flew past him, striking Cyrilla's back. She fell forward, and Berian twisted neatly out of the way. Something glittered in his hand. In a split second, he was facing Ryn again, his hand flying forward, a throwing star slicing through the air— straight past Ryn. Ryn heard Vi's sharp intake of breath, but his gaze didn't waver from Berian. He narrowed his eyes, aimed, and let the arrow fly.

It struck Berian in the chest. A second later, he hit the ground beside Cyrilla.

Ryn twisted around, fear gripping his heart, but Vi was still standing. Her chest heaved as she caught her breath, and she was barefoot. Her dress, which had previously been long enough to hide her feet, now ended above her knees. Well, that explained the ripping sound he'd heard. "You okay?" Ryn asked, suddenly noticing how oddly warm it was here. Some sort of protection from the elements, he figured.

"Yeah. Blade snagged my shoulder, but I'm fine. You?"

"Fine. I think. Aside from possibly being knocked on the head."

A moan caught his attention, and both he and Vi hastened toward the two fallen guardians. Within a minute, they were gagged and bound, guardian ropes glittering at their ankles and wrists.

With the arrows removed, it wouldn't take their bodies long to heal, but they'd be in Guild custody by the time that happened.

Ryn straightened and looked at Vi. Even in a torn dress with dirty smudges on her arms and her hair a loose, messy knot hanging just above one shoulder, she was beautiful. He kept the thought to himself, though. She would only roll her eyes if he told her. "Well," he said, grinning at her. "Hi. Fancy meeting you here."

"I know, right?" She heaved another breath and brushed dirt from her hands before placing them on her hips. She smiled at him. "You come here often?"

"Only to meet pretty girls in shredded dresses." His gaze moved pointedly to the ripped edge of her dress before returning to her face.

"What?" she demanded. "It was impractical and you know it."

"I didn't say anything."

"But you were thinking something."

"I'm thinking many things."

"You were thinking that I have a habit of ripping pretty dresses in half."

"Well ... you kinda do."

"I've done it *twice!*" she protested.

"This is the fourth time," Ryn corrected. "And who knows how many outfits you've assaulted while I haven't been around to keep count?"

Vi folded her arms. "Perhaps the Guild should stop sending me to cocktail parties and black-tie events."

"What the Guild should stop doing is finding work for both of us on date night. Now we have to call *this* our date." He gestured to the two struggling figures lying on the ground between them.

"Well, I suppose since we were both doing our favorite thing in the world—fighting bad guys—it wasn't too bad a date after all."

"I don't know about that," Ryn said with a small frown. "Fighting bad guys may have moved down the list for me in recent days. I can think of some other activities I'd rather be doing." He flashed her a knowing grin, and even in the soft light cast by the glow-bugs, he could see her cheeks flush.

"Are we interrupting something here?"

Ryn whipped around at the sound of the voice, his fingers already reaching for a weapon. But his brain caught up a second later, telling him it was a voice he knew. In the next moment, he recognized Asami and Jay stepping out of the faerie paths.

"Nope," Vi answered. "Just an average Friday night catching two guardians who turned out to be working with a drug-potion dealer."

Asami's frown deepened. "Someone alerted us to a disturbance here, and they said something about guardians fighting each other. We were hoping they were wrong." His eyes fell on Berian as he strode closer, and he pulled his head back in surprise. "Ryn, isn't this guy your partner?"

"Yep," Ryn said. "Seems he's been working *with* the drug dealer he and I were supposed to be hunting down. Not sure how Cyrilla ended up involved, but she seemed pretty keen on killing us."

Jay shook his head in disgust as he stared down at the struggling pair. "As if we haven't lost enough of our own already."

"Need help getting them back to the Guild?" Asami asked.

"Hey, Ryn?" Vi said before Ryn could answer Asami. He realized she'd moved a few paces away and was examining some of the flowers and trinkets arranged around the clearing. "I think we're standing in some sort of … memorial site."

He moved to her side, noticing folded notes, scrolls tied with ribbons, and pictures placed here and there among the other items. "That would explain why this area seems protected from the elements," he murmured. "Otherwise the flowers wouldn't survive the cold."

"I think … I think it's for people who were lost during and after The Destruction."

Her pain was sudden and overwhelming, piercing Ryn squarely in the chest. "Hey," he said, reaching for her hand. "You okay?"

With her eyes still fixed on one of the statues, she shook her head. She opened her mouth but no sound came out. After another few moments, she whispered, "Tora."

Ryn nodded and squeezed her hand. He'd guessed that was probably the cause of her abrupt emotion. Looking over his shoulder at Asami and Jay, he said, "Do you guys mind going ahead with them to the Guild? I'll meet you there in a few minutes."

"Sure thing, man," Asami said after a glance at Vi.

"Thanks." Ryn waited until they'd disappeared into the faerie paths with the two bound guardians hanging in the air between them, then shifted to wrap one arm around Vi's back. Together, they stood in silence.

CHAPTER 4

EMBARRASSMENT BURNED ALONGSIDE VI'S GRIEF AS SHE AND
Ryn stood among the memorial items. It went against everything
inside her to show any kind of weakness. She may have learned how
to let her guard down around Ryn, but in front of Asami and Jay?
No. She was supposed to be stronger than this.

"I'm sorry, this is so pathetic," she said, her voice shaky. "I'm
fine. We can head back to the Guild now. You need to deal with—"

"They can handle things for a few minutes," Ryn said.

Vi shook her head. "I'm sorry," she repeated, blinking furiously
at the tears that refused to recede. "Sometimes it just hits me out of
nowhere. Like … things feel almost normal, and you and I are
joking about something, and I forget that she's gone, and then
suddenly … *bam*. Something reminds me, and it's a shock all over
again. And then I think of everyone else who died, and I think of
my role in all of it—"

"Vi," Ryn said gently. He tipped her head up until she was
forced to meet his eyes. "*You* didn't kill those people. *You* didn't kill
Tora."

"But I helped."

53

"Unwittingly. And if you hadn't been around, Draven would have found someone else."

A short breath of a laugh escaped her lips. "If I hadn't been around, there never would have *been* a Draven."

"You can't keep doing this, V. We repeat this conversation every time."

"I know, I know." She released a frustrated sigh. "I'm sorry. I'm trying to move on. We had the ceremony, and we said goodbye to everyone, and that really helped, but still … some days are harder. Some days I fail. Some days it all feels so overwhelming and I don't know how I'll ever get past it."

Ryn pulled her closer and wrapped both arms around her. She rested her head against his chest, allowing a tear or two to travel down her cheeks. "Some days I fail too," he admitted. "There's so much pain, especially at the base with so many people living close together. So many overwhelming emotions I'm forced to feel every day alongside my own."

"I'm sorry." Vi squeezed her eyes shut and shook her head against Ryn's chest. The thing she hated the most about her grief was how selfish it made her, sucking her in and blotting out the rest of the world. "I know this is so much harder for you. Experiencing everyone else's suffering. I don't know how you handle it."

"Well," he answered, his tone lighter than before, "I'm awesome, so it comes naturally to me."

She rolled her eyes and managed a small laugh. "So humble."

"What were you doing tonight?" Ryn asked. "Before you showed up unconscious hanging over Berian's shoulder."

"Oh." She stepped back, suddenly remembering that she had her own assignment to finish off. "The art gallery."

"Right, and what were you doing there? Did you perhaps save someone's life? Prevent someone from getting hurt?"

"Well … I hope so. I wasn't there for long enough to find out, but I'm hoping my shield stopped a bunch of people getting punctured by shards of glass."

"And that's how we get past this," Ryn said. "All this grief and loss. We get past it one assignment at a time. One life at a time. One step at a time."

Vi focused on a tiny folded page with the name *Everly* written on it, the same dark thought that always tortured her creeping in at the edge of her mind: Would all the lives she saved ever make up for that one life she *hadn't* been able to save?

She blinked and banished the thought. "One step at a time," she said. "I know. You're right. Although …" She frowned. "Would there have been any shards of glass at all if Berian and I hadn't been there?"

Ryn shook his head. "Don't do that. You know it's pointless. It was one of the first things they told us back when we started training. You never know what may or may not have happened once you set about trying to change the future."

"Yeah, I know." Violet sighed and wiped the tears from her cheeks. She laced her fingers between Ryn's and met his gaze. At times it felt like those blue eyes were her only constant. She could stare into them and find exactly what she needed: understanding, warmth, security, love, mischief … It was far more than she would ever deserve.

"As much as I want to stay out in the forest with you all night," she said, "you need to get back to the Guild and deal with Berian and Cyrilla's arrest, and I need to rope in a few people and head back to the gallery to alter some memories."

"Yay date night!" Ryn said with an overly enthusiastic whoop.

Vi managed a genuine smile. Little did Ryn know that date night wasn't a complete bust just yet. If she could get him to hurry up at the Guild—and if she could finish up her own memory-wiping mission quickly—date night might actually go ahead. "You know, it's not that late yet," she told him. "Maybe there'll still be time to hang out once we're both done."

"Unfortunately not." Ryn's lips turned down. "The particular experience I had planned for tonight required us to be there at least an hour ago."

Vi raised an eyebrow. "Interesting. Well, as much as I appreciate all the surprises you like to plan—and I really, really do—not everything has to be a grand gesture or intricately planned series of events. Sometimes a simple date night on the couch is all we need."

"The couch, huh? I suppose I could roll with that."

Vi narrowed her eyes. "If you're about to add 'pun intended,' I will—"

"Hey, come on, I have more class than—"

They were interrupted by light streaking across the sky and a crack of thunder that sent shudders through the ground. Vi sucked in a gasp as her gaze snapped up toward the sky. Her heart thudded painfully fast. She met Ryn's gaze, and for just a moment, she saw the same fear mirrored in his eyes.

But a second later, logic caught up with her, and she remembered that Draven was gone and that storms were part of nature too, not just an evil overlord's arsenal. Suddenly, her gasp of horror seemed almost comical. She laughed as her shoulders relaxed. "I still have a moment of panic every time I hear thunder," she said.

Ryn's lips pulled into a crooked smile as he admitted, "You're not the only one. But we have nothing to worry about there. He's gone."

"Yes," Vi agreed. "He's gone." She nodded, and then Ryn nodded too, and then both of them were just silently nodding, waiting for the other to speak. She knew they were thinking of the same thing: The eternity necklace. The fact that Draven *might* have been wearing it. The fact that his body had disappeared. But they had talked about it before, and they would no doubt talk about it again, and they would probably never know what had truly happened to him.

So Vi took a deep breath and changed the subject. "Meet me back at the base when you're done?"

Ryn smiled. "Absolutely."

CHAPTER 5

VI SAT ON THE EDGE OF THE BED INSIDE HER SMALL BEDROOM at the Fireglass Vale base. Her left heel tapped repeatedly up and down, and her hands—which couldn't stop fidgeting with the zip of her jacket—were sweating. Did Ryn get this nervous every time he planned something in secret for her? Probably not.

She pulled Filigree onto her lap. He was currently in cat form with an impressive shock of fluffy white hair. Closing her eyes, Vi practiced some deep breathing while slowly dragging her fingers through Filigree's hair. She needed to get her galloping heart rate under control otherwise Ryn would know something was up before he even reached her room.

The slow breathing had just begun to work when a knock on her door sent her pulse through the ceiling again. Filigree yelped, and Vi realized her hands had unintentionally fisted in his long, lustrous hair. "Oh, sorry, Fili." She released him, laughing a little at herself as he climbed off her lap. She really was being silly. This was just a *date*. It was supposed to be fun.

But what if Ryn didn't like it?

She took another steadying breath. "Come in," she called as she stood, brushing cat hair off her pants. The door swung open to reveal Ryn standing there, and all thoughts of whether he might or might not like the date she'd planned fled her mind. The two of them were about to spend an evening together, and that was all that mattered.

Ryn leaned in the doorway and tipped his head to the side. "You're unusually excited to see me."

Vi shrugged in a way that felt far too forced as she walked over to him. "Maybe it's just been a really, really, *really* long day, and I'm glad I can finally relax with you."

"I see." A bemused expression crossed his face, which Vi took to mean that he did not, in fact, 'see.' But he looped his arms around her waist anyway and pulled her closer. "Did everything end off okay at the art gallery?"

"Yes. I think we found everyone who witnessed Berian and me disappearing into a dark hole in the air. It wasn't too complicated to make them forget. We didn't bother with those who saw the sculpture shatter. I'm sure they can come up with a non-magical explanation for that. And you? Done with Berian for now?"

"For now, yes. He'll be questioned tomorrow. And of course, the search for Elis Dei continues." Ryn let out a grim sigh. "I always suspected there was something off about Berian. I knew I never liked him."

Vi couldn't help her snort of a laugh. "Yeah, you never liked him because he's far too much like you."

"Oh *come on*," Ryn protested with a roll of his eyes. "Don't start with that nonsense again. He and I are absolutely nothing—"

"Arrogant, over-confident—"

"I am the picture of humility."

Vi laughed loudly, her nerves finally easing their grip on her insides. "You literally used the words 'I'm awesome' when talking about yourself earlier tonight."

Ryn pulled her closer and kissed the side of her mouth. "I was trying to make you smile."

"And you both think you're the best at everything."

"I don't think I'm the best at everything." He pressed a kiss beneath her ear and whispered, "I know that title belongs to you."

She laughed again, trying to smack him away as he continued a trail of kisses down her neck. It was a half-hearted effort though, because she was enjoying the kisses far too much.

"So," he said, pulling away and meeting her eyes just as she was about to lose herself in his embrace. "We're hanging out on a couch tonight."

She cleared her throat. "Right, yes."

"But your room doesn't have a couch, and my room doesn't have a couch, so …"

"So I guess we'll have to go looking for one."

"Lead the way then. Maybe we can …" He trailed off and looked down. "There's something—Oh, wow, Filigree. That is a *lot* of hair." Filigree, who was essentially all hair and no limbs, squeezed past Ryn's leg and sauntered off down the corridor as haughtily as a pillow of fluff could saunter. "Wow," Ryn repeated.

"I know," Vi said. "He's shedding everywhere. Anyway …" She removed her stylus from inside her jacket and opened a faerie paths doorway on the bedroom door. "We were on our way to find a couch." She reached for Ryn's hand and tugged him into the paths behind her.

As the edges of the doorway melted together, she turned to face him. His arms wound around her. Her lips found his in the darkness. "Don't think," she whispered against his mouth.

"Fine by me," he answered roughly, his hands twisting in her hair.

For several heart-pounding moments, Vi lost herself in the warmth of his lips, the tingle of magic on her tongue, the feel of his body molded against hers. But who knew where the heck they would wind up if one of them didn't tell the paths where to open, and so—with exceptional effort—she pulled her focus from Ryn's fingers trailing along the bare skin of her lower back and thought of her intended destination.

"We're here," she said as soft light brushed her eyelids and slow piano chords reached her ears. A husky female voice joined the piano's warm sound. She disentangled herself from Ryn's embrace and reached for his hand as they stepped out of the faerie paths. Concealed in a dark corner beside a bookcase, they looked out at the cozy room Vi had brought them to: mismatched tables and armchairs, shelves of old books with peeling spines, ancient type-writers, warm bulbs hanging from copper light fittings, and on the far side of the room, a raised stage where a woman was currently seated at a piano.

A waitress walked past with a tray holding two wineglasses and a mug of something that smelled like sweet, warm chocolate. The delicious aroma of freshly brewed coffee hung in the air, along with the spiced sweetness of baked goods.

"Where are we?" Ryn asked.

"A late-night cafe in a city that never sleeps. Human world, so zero overwhelming emotions. And it's slam poetry night, which I figured you'd enjoy, given your appreciation for poetry. And look." Vi pointed across the room. "There's a couch." She watched Ryn closely as he took in the scene, her anxiety easing as a smile spread slowly across his lips.

He looked at her, his eyes a sparkling, depthless blue. "So when you told me that a simple date night is all we need ..."

She lifted one shoulder. "You're always surprising me with something special—or planning to, at least, even if we've had to postpone our last few date nights—so I figured it was my turn to surprise you."

He slid one finger beneath her chin and tipped her face up toward his. The kiss he pressed to her lips was soft and lingering. Then he pulled his head back just far enough to ask, "Have I told you I love you?"

"You may have mentioned it once or twice. Have I told you I love you too?"

"Not sure. You might need to say it again, just to jog my memory."

She looped her arms around his neck and stood on tiptoe to whisper in his ear. "I love you, I love you."

He kissed her again, and there was a part of her that wondered if perhaps they should simply stay in this dark corner all night and forget the couch and the poetry and whatever delicious drinks were served in this place. But then the woman finished singing, and someone announced that the poetry performance would begin soon, and Vi figured that since they'd made the effort to get here, they probably shouldn't spend the *entire* evening making out.

She lowered herself to her heels, unwinding her arms from around Ryn's neck. "I think we can probably let go of our glamours. No one will notice us appearing out of thin air in this dark corner over here."

Ryn nodded. "Agreed. I wouldn't want to leave here without sampling whatever deliciousness they're baking back there."

"Come on." She slipped her hand into his. "Let's go grab that couch."

A TOUCH OF GOLD

This story featuring Tilly was written for the anthology *Once Upon A Quest* and is loosely based on the myth of King Midas and the Golden Touch, with a dash of inspiration from the tale of the Golden Fleece.

Read it any time after *The Faerie War*, Creepy Hollow Book Three.

CHAPTER 1

PLAYING A PART IN SAVING THE WORLD MADE EVERYTHING that came afterward a little boring in comparison. Which was why, on the day the two strangers showed up on the Floating Island of Kaleidos, sixteen-year-old Tilly was more than ready to pay attention.

It had been almost a year since a pair of guardians had come in search of her, carrying with them a prophecy and a sword. Almost a year since she'd helped bring an end to Lord Draven's reign before returning to her normal life. She'd spent every day since then longing for something just as thrilling to happen, and as sad as it sounded, the appearance of two strangers on Kaleidos was as close to thrilling as she was likely to get.

Kaleidos was suspended in the air above the sea, hidden from view by a layer of magic everyone called the shimmer. Most people in the world were unaware of the island's existence, so there weren't many who crossed the shimmer on a daily basis. In fact, Tilly probably came and went more often than anyone else. By unofficial means, of course. It was so much faster to take her brother's pegasus and fly over the wall encircling the island than to use the route everyone else used. That route involved getting permission from her parents—since she was underage—then going to the Travel Office built into the wall, presenting her permission slip, signing her name in the register, taking an airborne boat down to sea level, sailing just beyond the shimmer, and finally using the faerie paths to take her wherever she might want to go. Who had time for that?

"Okay *what?*" a woman said in the garden below. "Did that man seriously say *time* is different here?" It was one of the two strangers who spoke. They had just walked out of the Travel Office, and from her spot on the wall directly above them, Tilly could hear everything they said. School was on vacation, and she'd been lounging in the sun hoping for something interesting to happen when the two strangers—a tall, gangly man and a petite woman —arrived.

They stopped a few paces away from the wall, looking around at the colorful flowerbeds, the water feature near the edge of the Travel Office's garden, and in the distance, the small town surrounded by giant trees with homes nestled in the branches. "Yes," the man answered. "That is seriously what the travel official said." He unrolled the map he was carrying and squinted at it. "Sometimes time moves faster here on the island—which I *still* can't find on this map—and sometimes slower, with no pattern to the way it changes. Fascinating. Absolutely fascinating."

Tilly leaned toward the edge of the wall to get a better look at them. Upon closer inspection, she found they were younger than she'd first assumed. Almost as young as she was, perhaps. And like her, their two-toned hair indicated they were faeries. Tilly's was blonde and pink—a color she'd always found a little too girlish for her taste—while the two strangers had both been blessed with the beautiful combination of dark brown and warm caramel. And their skin … she'd never seen anything quite like it on a faerie. Bronze was the most accurate description, as it shone with an almost metallic sheen.

"I don't care that it's fascinating, Jayshu," the girl snapped. "It means we can't stay here. I thought this island would make a good hiding place, but—"

"It is a good hiding place. I doubt we'd ever have found it if we'd actually been *looking* for it. In fact, if I hadn't looked *up* at the right time and seen the shimmer, we probably would have sailed right past it and never been the wiser." He turned the map and examined it from a different angle. "I wonder why no one's ever been able to chart its exact—"

"Jayshu!" The girl snapped her fingers to get his attention. "Can you forget about your maps and books for just one minute and listen to me? What if we're here for one day and out there it's a week? Or more! They could get to the cave before we do."

Jayshu looked up. "Yadira," he said in a tone far calmer than hers. "They have no idea where the cave is. That's why they're chasing us, remember?"

Yadira groaned and turned away from him. "They'll probably find us here. They weren't far behind us on the sea, so I'm sure they'll be just as lucky as we were and see this island."

"Even if they do, it doesn't mean they'll find *us*. They don't know we're here." He paused before adding, "You didn't write your real name in that book, did you?"

"Of course not," Yadira answered. "But the baron will probably bribe that travel official into giving him the exact description of everyone who's arrived here today."

"Then let's put some distance between us and this office," Jayshu said as he rolled up the map. He swept one hand deftly over it, and in less time than it took Tilly to blink, the map was gone. With one last glance over their shoulders, he and Yadira left the Travel Office's garden and took the path that headed into town.

Tilly rose to her feet, tucked her short hair behind her ears, and hurried along the wall as quickly as she dared. A young man and woman on the run from someone called 'the baron'? And something about a secret cave? This sounded like an adventure she wanted to know more about. Perhaps if she offered Jayshu and Yadira a safe place to stay, they'd tell her more about it.

She jumped down, raced along a different path into town, darted past several buildings, and made for the path she knew Jayshu and Yadira were on. She saw them just as they strode into the town, heading for the Crystal Cafe. Tilly hurried to intercept them before they reached it, putting on her widest smile as she neared them. They glanced warily at her before diverting their gazes and walking a little faster toward Crystal Cafe's open door.

But they weren't as quick as Tilly. "Hi there," she said, stepping directly in front of them. "You guys are new, right? I saw you come through the Travel Office a few minutes ago."

Yadira's expression grew more guarded. "We're just visiting." She looked into the cafe and made as if to move past Tilly.

"Oh, wait, do you need someone to show you around?" Tilly took a step back before Yadira could pass her. "I can—"

"No thank you," Yadira said.

Tilly's eyes moved to the other stranger, Jayshu, but he was staring firmly at the ground. "Um, okay, so I'll admit I was sort of eavesdropping." Tilly twisted her hands together. "Okay, I was definitely eavesdropping. I know you're here because you're running away from someone, and I thought I might be able to help you."

At that, Jayshu finally looked up. His eyes were the same warm caramel as the streaks of color in his hair, but the look he gave Tilly was cold. He glanced away quickly and leaned closer to Yadira. "A trap, no doubt."

"I know, I'm not an idiot," she hissed.

"No, no," Tilly said. "This isn't a trap, I promise. I have no idea who's chasing you. I live here. I was hanging out on the wall, and I heard the two of you speaking, and I wanted to offer you a safe place to stay. My parents won't mind. They like meeting new people. I mean, as long as you're not here because of a prophecy that says you need to take me away to fight an evil dictator," she added with an eye-roll. "Then they'd probably turn you out." She laughed, a little too loudly perhaps, then forced herself to stop when she realized Yadira and Jayshu were still eyeing her with suspicion. "Um, sorry, that was a joke. The prophecy part. Not the first part. You really can stay with us if you need somewhere to hide. Our house is high up in one of the trees, and we even have a trapdoor in the floor because my dad makes faerie wine that's a tiny bit stronger than the legal limit, so he needs somewhere to hide it. But the space under the floor is big enough for two people to hide there. I can show you—"

A shout interrupted her. Yadira and Jayshu whipped around, and Tilly looked past them to see three men and a woman running along the path. "Oh no," Yadira whispered, stumbling backward into Tilly. "The baron."

"Run!" Jayshu said.

CHAPTER 2

"THIS WAY," TILLY TOLD THEM, ALREADY TURNING TOWARD the door behind her. "It'll be faster than going around." She ran into the cafe, where light reflected off the hundreds of crystals embedded in the walls and hanging from the ceiling. After racing between the tables, she barreled into the kitchen—and knocked right into Mrs. Plumleaf carrying a tray. Cupcakes flew into the air and froze before hitting the ground. "I'm so sorry!" Tilly gasped as she pushed past Mrs. Plumleaf. Reaching the door on the other side of the kitchen, she looked back for Yadira and Jayshu. They swerved to keep from running into her—just as bright sparks of magic flew over their heads.

They gasped and ducked down as Tilly's gaze snapped across the kitchen. One of the men who'd been chasing them had reached the doorway. Without thinking, she grabbed a knife from the nearest counter, pulled her arm back, and swung it forward. The knife landed with a dull whack in the doorframe, inches from the man's face. "Nice," Tilly said to herself, pleased she'd managed to strike the doorframe with the blade and not the handle. Then she spun back around. "Come on!" She threw her hand out, shoving the back door open with a blast of magic as

72

she lunged toward it. She raced outside, Yadira and Jayshu right behind her.

"I think we'll take you up on that offer to hide at your place," Yadira said as they ran.

Behind them, an explosion ripped through the air. Tilly looked around in time to see the cafe's back door land on the ground. "Actually ..." she said, facing forward and running faster. "New plan. You need to get off the island."

"But they'll stop us at ... at the Travel Office," Yadira panted as she struggled to keep up with Tilly. "I'm sure ... the baron will ... have left someone—"

"There's another way," Tilly said. "An unofficial way."

She raced between the buildings and gardens, sensing Yadira and Jayshu lagging behind her as she reached the edge of town. "Come on!" she called back to them. "We need to get to that forest beyond the giant trees."

"What about ... the faerie paths?" Jayshu grunted breathlessly.

"Can't access them on the island," Tilly shouted back. "Sorry!"

Their pace continued to slow as they passed the giant trees that held dozens of homes. But whenever Tilly looked back, the baron and his companions remained small figures in the distance. Clearly they were just as unfit as Yadira and Jayshu.

The three of them finally reached the forest. They continued running between the tall, spindly trees, though they were far slower now than Tilly would have liked. The trees eventually came to an end, and Tilly slowed to a halt at the edge of a lake. She took a few deep breaths before pursing her lips and whistling the signal to call Quartz. The pegasus lived in hiding here in the forest, since his presence on the island wasn't exactly legal.

"I seriously hope ... this wasn't ... some kind of trick," Yadira gasped.

"Trick?" Tilly turned back and found Yadira and Jayshu bent over, still trying to catch their breath. She was hurt that they still didn't trust her, but she had to remind herself that they barely knew her. "This isn't a trick. I'm offering you my brother's pegasus." As if on cue, Quartz chose that moment to step out of the trees further along the bank. He spread his wings, tossed his head, then folded his wings neatly against his body before walking toward Tilly. "See? Here he is. He's definitely big enough to carry both of you, so he can easily fly you off Kaleidos. Once you've found land, you can send him back. He'll know where to go."

Yadira straightened, her eyes widening. Beside her, Jayshu seemed just as uncertain. "Is that … safe?" Yadira asked.

"Of course it's safe. I leave this way all the time. Now hurry up before those people reach us. The saddle will materialize beneath you as you climb on."

"Okay," Jayshu muttered to himself as he stepped forward. "This is like riding a horse. You've done this before. It'll be fine."

"Exactly," Tilly said. "Just like riding a horse. But way up in the air instead. I mean, not that high," she added quickly as Yadira's eyes grew even wider. "Don't think about that part."

Jayshu pulled himself onto Quartz's back, and the saddle, enchanted to shrink or expand according to the number of people sitting on it, appeared beneath him. He helped Yadira up in front of him, and the saddle adjusted itself to fit her as well. "Okay, off you go," Tilly said, patting Quartz's shoulder and pushing aside her disappointment that this little adventure was already over.

But Quartz didn't move.

"Come on," Yadira said, squeezing her legs a little tighter around Quartz. "We need to go!" Instead of obeying, Quartz scratched at the sand with one hoof and tossed his mane.

Then, somewhere behind Tilly, the sound of hurried footsteps over forest debris reached her ears. She glanced back between the trees and saw movement. People running toward them.

"No, no, no," Yadira moaned. "He's going to catch us. Come on, pegasus, *move!*"

"He doesn't know us," Jayshu said. "Maybe that's why he won't leave."

Tilly's gaze snapped back to Quartz. "Maybe."

"Then come with us," Yadira said. "Quickly! We need to get away!"

Tilly paused for only a second, then climbed swiftly up behind Jayshu. "Let's go, Quartz!" she shouted. He whinnied, launched into the air, and the mighty beat of his wings carried the three of them up and away.

CHAPTER 3

KALEIDOS MUST HAVE BEEN CLOSER TO LAND THAT DAY THAN it usually was because Quartz reached the nearest beach in record time. Tilly slid off his back the moment he landed. "That was fun, right?" she said to the others as her feet sank into the loose sand.

Yadira climbed down and faced her. "Your aim with that knife was pretty good. You almost hit the baron."

"Oh yeah. Thanks. I've been practicing ever since—" She cut herself off, remembering she wasn't supposed to tell anyone about helping to defeat Lord Draven. That was something she'd achieved without possessing any skill in the fighting department, but she'd decided to change that upon her return to Kaleidos. She'd taken up magical defense at school, and in private, she began practicing with any weapon she could get her hands on. "Um … since … within the last year," she went on. "My aim's almost perfect now. The reason I didn't hit the baron is because I wasn't aiming for him. I could have, but I didn't want to stab the guy in the face. That would have been awful. I just wanted to startle him instead. Give us a few extra seconds to get away." She stopped when she noticed Yadira's perplexed expression. "Sorry. I talk a lot. I should probably return to the island now. Let you get on with your—"

"What's your name?" Yadira asked.

"Oh. I'm Tilly." She grinned and stuck her hand out to shake Yadira's as the other girl introduced herself.

"That knife-throwing thing …" Yadira said, tilting her head slightly as she lowered her hand. "Can you do other things like that? I mean, how good are you with other weapons?"

Tilly shrugged. "Slightly better than average, maybe?"

"Do you think you could fight a dragon?"

"Yadira," Jayshu said in a warning tone. He'd been rubbing Quartz's side, but now he looked over at his companion.

"A dragon?" Tilly repeated. "Wow, I have no idea. I mean, I've ridden one before, but he was really cool, so obviously I never fought him. And when you say 'fight,' do you mean kill? 'Cause I'm not down with that. But if you mean, like, defeat without injuring too badly, then maybe I could do that. I don't know."

"You rode one?" Yadira asked. "And you weren't scared of it?"

"No, of course not. Well, maybe a little in the beginning. But I got over that quickly."

Yadira nodded. She breathed in deeply, then said, "Come with us."

"What?" Jayshu said before Tilly could form a response.

Yadira turned to him. "We need a third person to help us with the dragon, okay? I've been thinking about it, and I highly doubt we can get past the dragon with only two of us. Tilly can help."

"Remember what you said after we escaped your house? About not wanting to call anyone we know for help? Not wanting to get anyone else involved?"

"Yes, I remember that, but I don't think we have a choice."

Tilly cleared her throat. "Um, get involved in what?"

Yadira stood a little straighter, her chin jutting forward as she faced Jayshu. "I'm going to tell her. You can't stop me." Jayshu turned away, hiding his expression. "I'm a maid in a baron's house,"

Yadira said to Tilly. "I've been there for eight or nine months, since Lord Draven's reign ended."

"Oh, interesting," Tilly said. "It's been closer to a year on Kaleidos." Then, at the sight of Yadira's raised eyebrows, she mimed zipping her lips shut and whispered, "Sorry."

"Anyway, someone got into his house recently and stole something of great value to him, and he blamed me for it. I had just returned to my home because I had the weekend off when he arrived with his men and a witch to question me. When I couldn't tell him what I'd done with this thing of great value, he threatened to kill me. I ran, and my cousin Jayshu—" she gestured over her shoulder "—helped me escape. But the baron has been chasing us ever since, and I think, hopefully—" she turned her gaze to the sky "—we've finally managed to get ahead of him."

Tilly had a number of questions by this point, starting with: "What is this thing that's so valuable?"

"It's …" Yadira hesitated a moment, perhaps wondering if she could trust Tilly with this information. "It turns things into gold."

Tilly's eyebrows jumped higher. "That sounds like powerful magic."

"It is. And the baron is a greedy man who wants to make himself even wealthier than he already is, and with his excess gold, he plans to bargain for things he shouldn't have. So we need to move this thing before he finds it."

"Okay, and is that where the dragon—Wait." Tilly narrowed her eyes. "You said you didn't take this thing, so how do you know where it is?"

Yadira sucked in a deep breath before speaking. "The truth is … I did take it. And it isn't a thing. It's a person. Mirradel. A woman the baron was keeping prisoner in his house. It's her touch that turns things into gold. When I discovered her locked in one of the highest rooms of the house, she begged me to help her escape, so I did."

Tilly closed her mouth, which had been hanging open for several seconds now. After another moment or two, she said, "This woman's touch can actually turn things into gold? That's incredible. That must be one of those special abilities, right? What are they calling them now? Griffin Abilities?"

"Yes, I think so," Yadira said.

"Wait, what does this have to do with a dragon?"

"After I helped Mirradel escape, I took her to the furthest place I knew of. A place I'd seen on one of Jayshu's maps. Then once we were there, we kept going. We went further than anywhere the faerie paths could take us. We found a cave, and I told Mirradel to hide there while I returned home for more food and other supplies. But just after I'd left, I realized the cave was home to a dragon. He was too big to fit inside the smaller cave further back where Mirradel was hiding, so I knew he couldn't get to her, but he wouldn't let me back in."

"And that's why you need help getting past a dragon," Tilly said, nodding now that it made sense.

"Yes. I believe it will take at least two people to successfully distract the dragon while one of us sneaks into the cave to get Mirradel out. And we need to go *now*, before the baron finds us again. He has a witch with him, and who knows what kind of tracking magic she might be capable of." Yadira paused, her gaze questioning and hopeful, before she asked, "So will you come with us?"

Tilly felt as if she were being torn in two. "I ... I can't. I want to —I really, *really* want to—but I can't cause my parents any more distress. I just about broke their hearts when I left without permission the first time. They thought maybe I'd died at Draven's hand, and when I returned, they didn't want to let me out of their sight for weeks. Once they started loosening up again, I began taking Quartz when my brother wasn't riding him, just so I could get off the island for short amounts of time and not go crazy with boredom. Sometimes I'm gone for an entire day or night if the time change is the wrong way. My parents freaked out the first time that happened, but now they know I'll always come back, so they just kinda put up with it. But this?" She shook her head. "I can't run off on an adventure that could take days. My parents will probably never forgive me for disappearing again, and then—" She stopped, breathing in deeply, realizing suddenly that she was doing the too-much-talking thing again. "Sorry. Too much information. But basically—" her shoulders drooped "—I can't go."

"But it won't take days," Yadira protested. "When we got to Kaleidos, the travel official said time was currently slower on the island than out here. He said five minutes on the island was close to an hour on this side of the shimmer, and that the most recent change occurred last night, so there shouldn't be another change for several more days."

"But he also warned us," Jayshu added, "that it's possible it could change at any moment."

"True," Tilly said, "but he has to say that. In reality, though, when there's a change it almost always lasts for at least four days. So if that's the case this time, then I should be fine. How long will it take to reach this dragon?" she asked Yadira.

"Not long. We can take the faerie paths to the furthest point I know of, and then it's only a few more hours by foot."

"Only a few more hours? Oh, that's perfect," Tilly exclaimed, her smile wide and her eyes shining. "As long as the time difference remains the same, barely an hour will pass on Kaleidos. My parents won't have to worry at all."

"Wonderful." Yadira clapped her hands in delight, her caramel eyes sparkling. Jayshu didn't seem convinced, but Tilly ignored him. She'd been waiting almost a year for something like this to happen, and now that she knew it wouldn't worry her parents, there was no way she was about to turn back home.

CHAPTER 4

YADIRA USED HER STYLUS TO WRITE A FAERIE PATHS SPELL IN
the sand. Moments later, the sand began to part, revealing a hole
with nothing darkness on the other side. Yadira held her hands out
for Tilly and Jayshu, and the three of them stepped into the paths.

They dropped downward, and then there was nothing for
several seconds—no sound, no light—until an uneven surface
formed beneath Tilly's feet. As their surroundings appeared and the
faerie paths closed behind them, Tilly found herself in a jungle.
Tangled trees and vines filled the scene, and the air, suddenly warm
and sticky, seemed to cling to her body. A stream crossed the
ground just ahead of her, tumbling over rocks and fallen branches.

"Okay," Yadira said, swatting at a small winged creature that
buzzed past her. "Look through the trees there." She pointed
beyond the stream. "Do you see that mountain peak in the
distance? The cave is at the base of that mountain, so that's where
we need to go."

"And you're sure we can't get any closer through the faerie
paths?" Tilly asked.

"Yes, I'm sure. I tried that before."

"Fascinating," Jayshu murmured. He walked ahead of them,

hopped across the stream using several boulders as stepping stones, and attempted to open a doorway to the faerie paths on the other side.

"Seriously?" Yadira said to him as she crossed the stream ahead of Tilly. "You don't believe me?"

"Just checking." Jayshu turned slowly on the spot. As Tilly reached the other side of the stream, he climbed onto a large rock and looked back the way they'd come. His map appeared in his hand. He examined it closely, looking up at his surroundings every few moments before returning his gaze to the unfurled scroll. "This is amazing," he said, sounding more animated than Tilly would have thought possible, given how grumpy he'd seemed so far. "We've gone right off the edge of the map." He jumped down from the rock and peered at the map once more. "The stream is right along here—" he tapped the border of the page "—and after that, the map simply ends. I think we truly are in uncharted territory."

"Incredible," Tilly breathed, leaning over the map to see exactly where it ended.

Jayshu took a startled step backward, snatching the map away. "Oh, uh, yes. Yes, very incredible. Uh, you said we're going this way?" he asked Yadira, but he was already turning and hurrying ahead before she could answer.

Tilly waited for him to be out of earshot before saying, "I don't think he particularly likes me."

She and Yadira began walking, and Yadira was quiet for a moment before she nodded. "Don't take it personally, though. He doesn't like most people. He'd rather spend his time reading books and studying maps and drawing pictures of landscapes and creatures and … stuff." Her voice grew quieter as she added, "I wish it hadn't been him who helped me escape, but he was the only one around when the baron showed up at my house. And the baron's been following us constantly since then, so it's been impossible to return home and get more help."

"Yeah, I suppose a bookish sort of person might not be the best companion when you need to fight a dragon," Tilly admitted.

"Oh. Yes. There is that. But what I meant was … well, Jayshu sort of creeps me out a bit. So I'm glad we found you, and I'm glad you know how to fight. I was worried Jayshu might try to—I don't know—attack me along the way and leave me somewhere. So he could keep Mirradel and her power for himself."

"*What?*" Tilly squeaked. "Jayshu? Attack you? He doesn't look like he could swat a nixle, let alone attack a person."

"I know, I know." Yadira shook her head. "I'm probably just being paranoid. Then again … they say it's usually the quiet ones, don't they?"

"What's usually the quiet ones?"

"Nothing. Never mind. I'm sure I'm being scared for nothing. He's definitely changed since we were children. I mean, I *think* he's changed. He's still so serious and moody, always wrapped up in his books, but at least he no longer seems to have that streak of …"

"Of what?" Tilly asked.

Yadira paused as the two of them bent to keep from being smacked in the face by a low branch. "It doesn't matter," she said. "It was long ago, and children don't always think properly. Their tempers are quick and they don't know how to control them. They end up doing silly things, you know?"

Something in Yadira's tone made it sound as though 'silly' wasn't the right word at all. Tilly laughed, hoping to lighten the mood. "That's certainly true. When my brother was young, he thought he was invincible. He thought he could walk along the thinnest branches at the top of our tree, and that he'd never fall. But he did, and he landed on our roof—thank goodness he didn't fall any further than that—and he broke his arm."

Yadira looked down and touched her right forearm. "I fell and broke my arm too," she murmured.

A shiver raised the hairs on Tilly's arms as she asked, "How?"

"It doesn't matter," Yadira repeated. "It wasn't really his fault, and it healed quickly."

"Uh, okay." Tilly swallowed her curiosity and managed to keep from questioning Yadira further.

"Come on, we need to walk faster," Yadira said. "Jayshu's getting too far ahead of—Ohmygosh!" She gasped and came to a complete standstill.

Tilly saw the giant serpent a split second later. It was almost as tall as she was when it reared its head up off the ground. Its glittering black eyes stared straight at her. "Hooooolycrap," Tilly said as she froze beside Yadira. "That thing is huge. Just … don't move."

"I—uh—I have a knife," Yadira stuttered, though she didn't move an inch. "If I can just … maybe … get to it, then I can give it to you."

"We have *magic*, Yadira! That's what we should be using right— Oooookay, it's moving closer." Tilly acted without thinking. She dove to the side just as the serpent's head flashed forward. She hit the ground—far less gracefully than a guardian, a detached part of her mind informed her—rolled over, threw both hands out, and watched as bright sparks sped away from her fingertips. Her magic struck the side of the serpent's face, knocking its head away from her.

She sat up, allowing herself to be pleased for a moment that she'd successfully managed to use offensive magic. But she was still on the ground, and the serpent was rearing back around, hissing as smoke rose from a wound beneath its eye. Crumbs, was its flesh actually *burning*? Guilt welled up inside Tilly. Guilt that was immediately extinguished when the serpent bared its oversized fangs at her and lunged—

Another spark of light flashed straight toward the serpent, striking the back of its head. The serpent writhed and twisted, then slithered quickly past Tilly. She scrambled away from it, but the creature no longer seemed interested in attacking her. She looked up toward the source of the second magical attack and found Jayshu standing there, one hand extended and a look of shock on his face. "Whoa," he said. "Did I actually hit that thing?"

"You did," Tilly said as she climbed to her feet. "Thank you. I might have been a serpent snack otherwise, and my parents *so* would not have appreciated that. Not that they would ever have known. Which is even worse, I suppose." She shook her head. "Okay, let's not be so preoccupied." She looked at Yadira. "We need to be ready to react instantly with magic. That's what guardians do, right?"

"Why didn't you kill it, Jayshu?" Yadira snapped, ignoring Tilly.

Jayshu's almost-smile evaporated. "Well, I figured scaring it away would be just as effective. No need to go around killing things unnecessarily."

"This *was* necessary, Jayshu. What if it comes back?"

"Then we'll just have to scare it off again," Tilly said, walking forward. "Or we can keep moving, faster than before, and hope it doesn't catch up to us again."

"Fine." Yadira exhaled slowly. "Yes, you're right. I'm sorry."

The three of them remained together after that, moving as swiftly as they could through the jungle. By the time they neared the base of the mountain, the sun had just about disappeared behind it. "Quietly now," Yadira said to them. "We're almost at the cave. The dragon might be able to hear us."

Tilly placed her feet more carefully against the ground, but she couldn't completely silence the snap of twigs and the crunch of damp earth beneath her shoes. An icy finger of fear traced across the back of her neck as an unseen creature let out an eerie cry somewhere nearby.

"Stop." Yadira put her hand out, halting Tilly and Jayshu. She pointed between the trees. "There he is."

A few paces ahead of them, the trees came to an end. A narrow river cut across the ground just beyond that, and on the other side yawned a large opening in the rocky mountain face. In the shadow of the cave mouth sat a dragon. Vibrant green scales covered its body, and its unblinking eyes—which seemed to be pointed in their direction—were a fiery orange.

"He never sleeps," Yadira whispered. "I watched him for a long time when I was here before, and he stayed awake the entire time. Not once did he leave the cave."

Tilly looked at her. "How do you know it's a 'he'?"

"Because—" Yadira frowned. "I don't know. It just seems like a he."

"If he never leaves," Jayshu said, "then how did you and Mirradel get inside in the first place? He must have left it unguarded at some point."

"It was unguarded at first," Yadira said, a hint of exasperation in her voice. "But once the dragon returned and discovered there was someone inside the cave, he refused to leave. I told you, I watched him for a long time. Don't you believe me?"

"I do," Jayshu said. "I just wonder if he might leave again."

"We don't have time to wait and find out," Yadira replied. "We can't risk the baron catching up to us."

Jayshu sighed. "Fine. I suppose I'd better get ready to face a dragon then."

Tilly couldn't help smiling. "Awesome," she whispered to herself. "Bring it on, Mr. Dragon."

CHAPTER 5

TILLY AND JAYSHU REMAINED HIDDEN AMONG THE TREES while Yadira headed further along the river toward one of the boulders that sat right on the riverbank. The plan was for her to hide behind the boulder and then signal Tilly and Jayshu to jump out and try to draw the dragon away from the cave mouth while she snuck across the river and into the cave. Hopefully, with two of them to fight back with magic instead of one, Tilly and Jayshu wouldn't wind up burned to a crisp before Yadira managed to rescue Mirradel.

"I can do this," Jayshu whispered to himself as he and Tilly watched the dragon. "I can be brave. I can fight a dragon."

"Of course you can," Tilly said, almost reaching out to pat his shoulder before deciding he probably wouldn't like that. "*We* can. It's just a dragon, right? How hard can it be?"

He laughed then—actually laughed—a rich sound that warmed Tilly's chest. He stopped abruptly, though, seeming to remember who exactly he was laughing with.

"You don't like me, do you," Tilly said with a sigh.

"What? I—uh—why would you—" He cleared his throat, still refusing to look at her. "Why would you think that?"

87

"Uh ... perhaps because you don't want to talk to me? Or because you won't even look at me?"

"I'm ... just ..." Jayshu scratched the back of his neck before forcing himself to meet Tilly's eyes. "Shy," he finished quietly. "Very shy. Around new people."

"Oh." Tilly paused, then grinned. "Oh, awesome. That's so much better. I can work with shy. At least I know it's not that you don't like me."

He laughed again, though it was quieter now, and he still seemed reluctant to look at her. "I think it's far more likely that you're about to find out *you* don't like *me*. I'm not ... well ... brave." He stared at the ground, which Tilly realized probably made it easier for him to talk to her. "I've always longed to be braver than I really am." The words tumbled quickly from his lips, as if he were confessing a secret. "I've read stories of great heroes and their exciting adventures. I've always dreamed of being that kind of person, but now that I've found myself on my own mini adventure, I have to admit it's pretty darn terrifying. I don't think I've ever done anything brave before. Well, there was that time Yadira ended up trapped by a giant spider when we were on holiday and there was no one else around, so I had to save her. No, wait, I was terrified then too. Completely terrified. The poisonous bite didn't help."

Thrilling images raced through Tilly's mind. "A giant spider? Those are real? And it *bit* you?"

"Yes. I was so mad at Yadira afterward. I'd been telling her not to go into that tunnel, and she kept teasing me about being scared of the dark. She ran in anyway, and she fell into a spider's lair and broke her arm. I almost froze completely when I saw the size of that spider, but I told myself I had no choice. I had to get her out. I managed to save her, though I realized once we reached safety that the spider had bitten my leg. Anyway, magic healed it up pretty quickly." He stopped, blinked at Tilly, then looked away again. "Sorry. Mostly I don't say much, but I babble when I'm nervous."

Normally, Tilly would have jokingly replied with something like, "At least you don't babble *all* the time, like I do." But her mind was turning back to Yadira's story about being afraid of Jayshu and implying some sinister connection between him and her broken arm. But perhaps Tilly had misunderstood what Yadira meant. "Was that the only time she broke her arm?" Tilly asked carefully.

"I think so. Our families have always lived close to one another, so I'm sure I'd know if she'd broken her arm more than once."

"Oh. Okay." Tilly chewed her lip, watching for signs of Yadira's stealthy progress toward the boulder. Why had the girl lied to her about Jayshu? Or could it be possible Jayshu was the one lying? That didn't seem right, though. Tilly felt as if the conversation they'd just had was genuine.

"Anyway, back to the point," Jayshu said. "I'm nothing like those heroes I've read about. I was afraid then, and I'm afraid now."

Tilly frowned. Her gaze moved from the river to the dragon, whose burning orange eyes made her pulse quicken with fear. "But … that's kind of the point isn't it? When you face the thing you're afraid of, that's what makes you brave."

Jayshu was silent a moment before saying, "I suppose it does. Oh, look, Yadira just signaled us." He pushed his shoulders back and swallowed. "Right. Okay. Let's do this."

They both took a deep breath, and then together, the two of them ran out of the trees toward the river, waving their hands and shouting. They no doubt looked ridiculous, but there was no way the dragon would miss them. "It's working," Tilly said as the dragon rose onto his feet. "Be ready to run," she added. "And to throw magic or shield yourself from the flames."

As if he could hear her, the dragon reared up and let loose a stream of fire toward the treetops. Then, with a snarl, he lunged across the river.

Straight at Yadira.

CHAPTER 6

"No!" Tilly yelled. "This way!" She jumped up and down, waving her arms about, while Jayshu rushed forward and splashed into the river. After one more shout, Tilly gave up and hurried after him. Both Yadira and the dragon were in the river, which was about waist-high at its deepest point, and wasn't flowing particularly fast. Yadira was doing her best to shield herself from the dragon's flames, but Tilly could see heat shimmering in the air where the layer of shield magic had begun to weaken.

Jayshu threw a handful of sparks at the dragon, but Tilly held her magic back. A few sparks wouldn't do anything against a beast so large. They needed something more. She'd read about magic that was powerful enough to knock a person or creature unconscious. A stunner spell, it was called. And while there was no way she had time to gather the kind of power necessary to stun a dragon, she might be able to gather just enough to push him away from Yadira.

She reached the other side of the river and ran, dripping wet, up the bank, constantly drawing on the core of magic deep inside her. Between her hands, an orb of power began to form. It flashed and sparkled and struggled to break free. Still in the river, Jayshu continued tossing various forms of magic at the dragon, which at least gave Yadira a chance to reinforce her shield magic. But after a particularly large blast of flames forced Jayshu to dive beneath the water, Tilly decided she'd waited long enough. She raised her magic above her head with both hands and threw it with all her might at the dragon's head.

Her aim was true, and her power was greater than she'd thought. It struck the side of the dragon's face, knocking his head away from Yadira. His thick neck swung sideways, and his head cracked against a rock on the riverbank.

Tilly froze. So did Jayshu and Yadira.

Was the dragon still conscious? Had she actually managed to injure him?

Then he shook his head before slowly turning to face her. His orange eyes burned into hers, and she wondered for one paralyzing moment if he had the power to hypnotize her.

Then something solid slammed into her abdomen, sweeping her completely off her feet. The dragon's tail, she realized belatedly as she flew through the air. *Stop, stop, stop!* she yelled silently, throwing magic out beneath her, hoping to cushion her fall. She managed to slow herself, but pain still blazed throughout her body when she hit the ground.

It took her several moments before she was able to sit up. Then another few moments before she pushed herself onto her feet. She was about to run back toward Jayshu and Yadira when she realized something: The dragon had moved far enough from the cave that she could easily slip inside unnoticed. She looked back to make sure Jayshu and Yadira were still managing to fend off the dragon, then ran through the opening in the side of the mountain.

The dim light of early evening illuminated the interior of the cave, revealing another opening at the far end. As Tilly grew closer to it, she noticed golden light streaming faintly through it into the cave she currently stood in. Her heart leaped, and she hurried forward.

She knew the moment she stepped into the second, smaller cave that she'd found the right place. By the light of several enchanted candles floating near the ceiling, she saw gold stones scattered across one side of the cave. Some of the vines that had found their way inside were gold too, and in the center of the cave sat a gold backpack.

But her amazement turned to horror when she saw the woman pressing herself against the far wall. Her dress was torn and dirty, and a small cage-like structure enclosed each hand. "Oh no, that's awful!" Tilly exclaimed. "Who did that to you? Did someone else find you here?" She rushed forward to help the woman.

"No! Stay away." She shrank further back against the wall.

"Hey, Mirradel, it's okay." Tilly stopped and held her hands up to show she meant no harm.

"You know who I am?" Mirradel asked.

"Yes. We came here to get you out. I swear I'm not here to hurt you or use your power."

"Even if that's true, you shouldn't come near me. If you touch my hands, you'll be turned to gold. I had gloves—enchanted gloves that didn't become gold when I put them on—but they were destroyed when I was captured." A small winged creature—a sprite, Tilly realized—landed on Mirradel's shoulder holding what looked like an armful of berries.

"Oh, that's clever," Tilly said, taking a tentative step forward. "Has the sprite been feeding you? Since you can't use your own—"

"Get the hell out of here!" Mirradel shrieked, looking past Tilly. "I refuse to turn anything else into gold for you!"

Tilly's heart pounded as she swung around, expecting to find herself face to face with the baron.

But it was Yadira who stood there.

CHAPTER 7

"YOU?" TILLY SAID, HER BROW SCRUNCHING UP AS SHE struggled to figure out what was going on.

"Yes," Yadira said. "Me." She held a knife in one hand, while magic crackled around the other. "Now get out of the way."

"Wait. Your entire story was a *lie*?"

Yadira cocked her head. "Actually, most of my story was true. The only part I had to twist was the beginning. I didn't rescue Mirradel from her captor; I *stole* her from her husband. I mean, just look at what she can do." Yadira gestured to the gold items around the cave. "Don't tell me you wouldn't want this gift for yourself."

"That wasn't your only lie," Tilly said between gritted teeth. "You lied about Jayshu too. About being afraid he might attack you, and implying he hurt you as a child. Why would you say things like that?"

Yadira shrugged. "I was just embellishing facts. It was fun. I didn't plan for either of you to make it out of here alive, so it didn't matter to me what you believe about him."

"Then why bother bringing me with?"

She sighed. "Jayshu's useless. I didn't trust him to keep the dragon occupied for long enough to allow me to get in and out of the cave. You seemed a little more capable."

Fear sent a chill through Tilly's body. "Where is Jayshu? What did you do to him?"

Yadira's lips turned up in a cruel smile. "You shouldn't be worried about what *I* did to him. Perhaps you should run along outside and find out what that dragon's doing to him."

Mirradel let out a yell, and before Tilly realized what was happening, the woman with the golden touch had launched herself across the cave at Yadira. "Stop ruining people's lives!" she yelled as she swung her caged hands at Yadira's face. "Who do you think you are?"

Bright light shot away from Yadira's hand. A moment later, Mirradel hit the floor with a groan. One of the cages snapped open and fell away from her hand.

"Are you okay?" Tilly gasped, running toward her.

"Ugh, stop interfering," Yadira said. She raised the knife, aimed at Tilly, and threw—

"No!" someone shouted.

Mirradel lunged across the floor, her hand reaching for Yadira's ankle, just as Tilly threw herself out of the knife's path. It nicked her shoulder and clattered to the floor—and in the same instant, Yadira became a solid gold statue.

"Oh my goodness," Tilly whispered, staring wide-eyed at the girl's golden face, frozen forever in an expression of surprise. Then her gaze shifted beyond the statue, to where Jayshu stood in the cave's doorway, his clothes partially singed and his hand outstretched just as it had been after he'd thrown magic at the serpent. "I hit her," he murmured. "My knife hit her. And then she turned to gold." Tilly stepped slowly around the statue and saw that he was right. Buried between Yadira's shoulder blades was a golden knife.

Mirradel sobbed into her free hand. "I didn't want ... to hurt ... anyone else."

And for only the third or fourth time in her life, Tilly had no idea what to say.

"Mirradel!" a new voice called out from somewhere behind Jayshu. Tilly looked past him and saw a man—the man who'd chased them across Kaleidos—hurrying into the cave. "My love, I'm so sorry." He ran toward Mirradel. "I got here as soon as I possibly could."

"Wait, be careful," she said before he could get too close. "My gloves. Yadira destroyed them when she took me."

"I know. I saw them on our bedroom floor. That's why I brought—"

"Cecile!" Mirradel cried out as a woman rushed into the cave along with the other two men who'd been chasing Yadira and Jayshu. "I'm so glad you're here."

Tilly managed to stifle her gasp at the sight of the woman's black eyes and pointed teeth. She'd never heard a single good thing about a witch, but perhaps some of them weren't that bad.

"Of course I'm here," Cecile said, her voice surprisingly gentle. "I won't let you suffer from this gift any longer than necessary." As Mirradel stood, she added, "Come outside and put your hands in the river. I'll make you a new pair of gloves."

"I'm—I'm so sorry," Jayshu stammered, his gaze on the ground as he stepped aside to let Mirradel pass. "I had no idea. Yadira said you were the baron's captive. I never would have helped her if I'd known the truth."

"It's okay," Mirradel sniffed. "She deceived us all." She looked around the cave and added, "You can take as much of this gold as you wish. Or don't take any of it at all, if that's what you'd prefer. It's up to you."

"Oh, um—thank you," Tilly said. Her eyes swept across the

cave, wondering exactly how much wealth it currently contained. "Perhaps just one or two stones. I don't want to be greedy." She had a feeling that taking anything more might lead her down the same path Yadira had ended up on.

CHAPTER 8

As everyone else left the cave, Tilly turned to Jayshu. "So, uh … what happened with the dragon?"

"Funny thing, actually. I remembered an enchanted lullaby my mom used to sing to me when I was little. Every single time, I'd fall asleep the moment she finished the last word. Turns out it works on dragons too."

Tilly blinked. "You really should have thought of that sooner."

"I know." Jayshu looked down, then peered up at her from between his lashes. "Anyway … the unexpected bonus of facing a dragon is that talking to you seems a lot less scary now than it did earlier today."

A smile spread across Tilly's face. "That's a definite bonus."

"So …" He raised his eyebrows. "I guess you need to go back home now?"

Tilly sighed. "I guess. What about you?"

"I'm planning to come back here, actually. I'll search for any record of whether this area has been mapped before, but I honestly don't think it has been. I want to explore it further and record whatever I discover."

"Alone?" Tilly asked. "That doesn't sound particularly safe."

"Oh." Jayshu frowned. "True. I suppose I should probably assemble some sort of team. People with expertise in different areas. Is that how exploration is done?" He gave her one of his rare smiles. "This is all very new to me, but I've suddenly realized it's exactly what I want to do. I want to be the person who draws the very first map of a brand new place instead of being the person who studies that map later on. And I want to—well—practice being brave."

Tilly gripped both his hands tightly in hers, her eyes shining as excitement welled up inside her. "I want to go with you," she said, the words tumbling hurriedly from her lips. "Not yet. I can't do that yet, and the thought is almost killing me, but I have a year and a half left of school, and I can't break my parents' hearts again. I'd feel guilty for the rest of my life if I did. But once I'm finished and I'm old enough to choose what to do with my life, I want to join you. Please." She squeezed his hands a little tighter. "I can do—well, anything you need me to do. I can fight whatever threatening forces we come across in the uncharted areas of the world, or I can learn any other skill you need me to learn, and we can explore together. I mean, with whatever team you've assembled by then. It'll be the best and biggest adventure *ever*."

Jayshu's smile turned into an actual grin. "That sounds like a brilliant plan. I can't wait."

THE PROPOSAL

This story takes place two years after *The Faerie War*,
in between the end of Violet's part of the Creepy Hollow series
and the beginning of Calla's part of the series.

Read it any time after *The Faerie War*,
Creepy Hollow Book Three.

CHAPTER 1

"Rejected," Jamon said, walking into the Underground living room where Vi, Ryn and Natesa were already sitting. He tossed a scroll onto the table and flopped into an armchair. "It's official. Kesh just received word."

"I'm so sorry," Natesa said, reaching for his hand.

On the couch beside Violet, Ryn leaned forward on his knees with a defeated sigh. "I thought you might actually have a chance this time."

"I don't understand," Vi said, her hands clenching tightly in her lap. "I honestly thought they were open to the idea this time. That councilor I spoke to said they were presenting the idea favorably to the Seelie Court, and other guardians were looking into the weapon spells, and—"

"That's the basis for the Guild's refusal this time," Jamon said, jerking his chin at the scroll. "The fact that it's faerie-specific magic and would never work on reptiscillas or other fae. Utterly ridiculous, but there you have it."

"You don't think they're lying, do you?" Natesa asked.

"No, but I don't believe they can't adjust the spells to make them appropriate for reptiscillas. This seems too much like a convenient excuse."

Vi nodded, her eyes remaining fixed on her lap. "I think you're right. Remember what Uri said?"

Jamon nodded, and Natesa looked over at Vi. "What did he say?"

"I spoke to him early in the process when they were still investigating the magic involved in guardian markings. He said that at best, the markings would be useless on reptiscillas. At worst, they'd be lethal. But he seemed to think it would be possible to come up with similar magic appropriate for reptiscillas."

"I'm sure they could figure it out if they wanted to," Ryn said, sitting back with a sigh. "The problem is that they don't."

"Exactly," Vi said.

Jamon nodded. "Which tells me that the Guild will deny our request every single time, no matter how many petitions we lodge." He shook his head. "Dammit, I've put so much into this, and it's all come to nothing."

"I know," Ryn said. "You even gave up leadership for this."

Vi elbowed him and gave him a look that was meant to say, *Seriously? That's not helpful.*

Jamon, however, simply laughed. "That was hardly a sacrifice. You know I never really wanted to be Leader Supreme. Good old cousin Kesh does a far better job than I would have done. Besides, this way I get to spend the rest of my life with someone I *want* to be with instead of being forced into a union with some other Leader Supreme's daughter." He smiled at Natesa, and she stretched across the space between them to give him a quick kiss. Glossy black hair braided with colorful ribbons slid over her shoulder, shielding their faces for a moment.

"What will you do now?" Ryn asked as Natesa leaned back in her seat, her hand still in Jamon's.

"I don't know. This has been my focus ever since we got rid of

Draven. All I've wanted is to see reptiscillan guardians out there making a difference to the world in the same way faerie guardians do."

Vi sat forward, excitement buzzing through her body as an idea suddenly occurred to her. "Then you must do it. *You* must make it happen. Screw the Guild."

"Vi," Natesa murmured, no doubt objecting to Vi's language.

"Sorry. Seriously, though, just forget about the Guild. Who says you can't do this on your own? If it's possible to get this kind of magic to work for reptiscillas—or to create spells that are similar— then do it without their help. Start your own version of a Guild."

Jamon rubbed a hand across his jaw. "That's not a bad idea ... except for the fact that I don't have a clue how to create new spells or enchantments, or even how to manipulate existing ones."

"So find someone who does."

"And we'd still need approval from the Seelie Court, I assume, if we're hoping to act on behalf of the Law."

"Well, you won't know unless you ask. Perhaps the Seelies would be open to a separate system of law enforcement instead of trying to blend you guys with an existing one."

"And what about the actual training?" Jamon asked. "I'm not sure I'd know where to begin with that. I mean, setting up an entire Guild-like system ... that's huge."

"I could help you. I mean, you know, if you want to employ me," Vi added with a smile.

"Seriously?" Jamon leaned forward. "You'd leave your Guild to come and work at mine?"

"Yes. I'm so sick of their stuck-up ways. They were desperate during Draven's reign, so they accepted help from anyone who could fight, but now they're back to thinking they're better than everyone else."

"Not everyone feels that way," Ryn said quietly.

Vi glanced over at him, but he was staring at the floor with a frown and didn't look up to meet her gaze. "Well, no," she said, "but enough of them do."

"It's a massive undertaking," Jamon said, "but we have no other option, so … perhaps we should try."

"Of course you should try," Natesa said, her expression bright. "Of course you can do this. Vi and Ryn will help, and there are others at the Guild who've been on our side since the first petition."

Vi watched a smile growing on Jamon's face, knowing he was warming up to the idea. "Yeah. We can do this."

Ryn cleared his throat. "Uh, we picked up dinner on the way here, Jamon. Brownie's just opened a branch at the shoppers' clearing."

The subject change was abrupt, but before Vi could comment on it, Natesa jumped up and said, "Oh yes, I'll get it." Vi tried to catch Ryn's eye, but he seemed to be avoiding looking her way. "It's great having a Brownie's Munch Box here in Creepy Hollow," Natesa said, placing the various boxes of food onto the table beside the half-crumpled scroll Jamon had tossed there. "Three months into our union, and apparently I still can't produce dinners that match up to Jamon's mom's."

"Hey, I never said that," Jamon protested.

Natesa rolled her eyes. "You didn't need to. Your half-hearted 'Mm, delicious' gives you away every night, and you're always far too enthusiastic when your mom invites us over for dinner."

"Maybe I'm just … happy to visit my mom."

"Right." Natesa laughed as Jamon leaned forward to help her open all the boxes. "I'm pretty sure Brownie's does a better job than I do, so I think we'll have to eat from there more often. Vi, I hope you don't have this problem when you and Ryn eventually get married," she added with a sly grin.

Warmth flooded Vi's chest—and most likely her face too, if the burning in her cheeks was anything to go by. Natesa was always trying to get Vi to tell her when she and Ryn planned to make their relationship a permanent arrangement, but she generally didn't bring it up in front of Ryn as well. Though Vi had certainly *thought* about spending the rest of her life with him, they hadn't had any serious discussions about it. There had been so many things to do after Draven was defeated, and now, with everyone's lives having finally settled into a new kind of normal two years later, their work at the Guild kept them more than a little busy.

Deciding to take a lighthearted approach to Natesa's comment, Vi said, "Nah, I plan to let Ryn cook every meal, so we'll be fine." She threw a smile over her shoulder at him, but he was still avoiding her gaze. Unease tugged at the edge of her mind, and her smile slipped a little. She found herself wishing, not for the first time, that she had his ability instead of her own. He wasn't the moody type, so if something was upsetting him, it was probably serious. If she could feel what he was feeling, she might understand what the problem was.

"Doesn't Ryn cook all your meals already?" Jamon asked with a teasing smile. "He's super romantic like that, isn't he?"

Ryn leaned over the side of the couch and punched Jamon's arm, but he was smiling now, and it almost looked genuine. "I would—if we ate more meals together. But work often gets in the way."

Jamon took the plate Natesa held out to him. "You guys would get to see more of each other if you just moved in together. No need to jump straight to a union ceremony if you're not ready for that."

Ryn nodded as he picked up the nearest container of food and examined the label. "That's what I said."

"And scandalize the whole of Creepy Hollow with our inappropriate living arrangements?" Vi asked in a tone of mock horror.

"That's what *I* said," Natesa threw in. "The older fae generations are super conservative."

"It's not as though you've ever worried about what people think of you," Ryn said to Vi. He looked at her now, holding her gaze in a way that suggested he wasn't joking the way the rest of them were. The smallest of frowns pulled at his brows. He didn't seem *upset*, exactly. More … thoughtful?

Natesa caught Vi's eye and gave her a questioning look. Vi lifted her shoulders in a quick shrug before neatly changing the subject to the upcoming Liberation Day Ball.

* * *

A few hours later, as Vi and Ryn stepped from the faerie paths into the forest near the small home Vi had shared with her father since she moved out of Fireglass Vale, things still weren't right. Ryn held her hand loosely in his, his thumb rubbing up and down against her skin in a way he probably wasn't even aware of.

He'd been quieter than usual this evening, but the fact that he'd brought them out of the faerie paths into the forest and not inside Vi's home suggested he was ready to talk now. Vi could have told him that her father wasn't home—working at the Seelie Court meant he only had a few days off every month, and today wasn't one of them—but she liked being in the forest. She and Ryn usually had their best conversations out here, nestled somewhere beneath whispering leaves and chirping night creatures.

She tugged his hand and pulled him to a stop. "What's going on?"

He hesitated a moment before answering. "Have you thought about this at all, this reptiscillan Guild thing, or was it a spur-of-the-moment idea?"

"Oh." That's what had been worrying him? "It was definitely spur-of-the-moment, but the more I think about it, the more excited I get."

"Really? So you've considered everything?" His blue eyes pierced hers with an intensity she didn't quite understand. "You've thought about having to give up your weapons, having your marks deactivated, having nothing to do with our Guild anymore? Being a guardian is what you've worked so hard for all your life, and now you're going to give it up?"

Vi paused. She let go of Ryn's hand and twisted a strand of hair around her finger. "Okay, so I hadn't thought about all of *that*." A pang twisted her insides at the thought of never entering a Guild again. "But … maybe the Council will be happy to let me remain a guardian while working with Jamon."

"Really?" Ryn's tone was doubtful. "You think they'll be happy with that?"

"I don't understand," she said with a frown. "I thought you'd *like* this idea. You've been just as supportive of Jamon's petitions to join the Guild as I have."

"I know, but …" Ryn ran a hand through his hair, his gaze shifting away from hers. "You leaving the Guild … that just came out of nowhere."

"Well, not really. You know I'm not entirely happy there. Nothing is the way it was before The Destruction. Tora isn't there, and everyone's turning against the fae who helped us fight Draven's followers. Plus there's the way everyone treats the—what are they calling them now? Gifted? Griffin Gifted? It's just not the same Guild I worked so hard to be a member of. If I think about it, there isn't really anything I'd be heartbroken to leave."

Ryn leaned away from her, brows raised and hurt evident in his eyes. "Nothing? Not even me?"

Oh. *Oh.* Finally she understood why he was upset. She took his hand again and tried not to laugh at the ridiculous conclusion he'd arrived at. "I wouldn't be leaving *you* by leaving the Guild. Besides, you'd come with me, wouldn't you? I know you'd rather work with reptiscillas than stuck-up guardians. In fact, I'm pretty sure you've said those exact words at least once in the past year."

"It doesn't matter what I want, Vi. The Guild runs the justice system of our world. We have a responsibility to know what they're doing and how they're doing it. I can't just leave. And if you're not there anymore, it means we'll hardly see each other."

"But … we're not even on the same team, Ryn. It's not as though we see each other a great deal as it is."

"But I do see you. If you're working in someone else's Guild, I'll *never* see you. Isn't that something that bothers you?"

"I—of course it does, but—"

"But it isn't something you even considered."

"Well, no, because I can't imagine a world in which we never spend any time together. That kind of world doesn't exist for me. We'll make it work somehow."

"Somehow?" His hand slipped out of hers, leaving her fingers feeling cold. "You barely have any time off as it is. Do you really think that's going to change when you're helping set up an entirely new Guild system?"

"I'll *make* time to see you, Ryn."

"Will you? It's not as though you make time now. Why will things be any different when you leave the Guild?"

Hurt pierced her chest. She wrapped her arms around herself, as if that could heal the ache. "How can you say that? We *both* work a lot. We both have difficulty making time for each other. Don't put this all on me."

He dragged both hands through his hair before letting them fall to his sides. "I'm sorry. I know, I'm sorry. I just … I end up missing you so much by the end of the day, and then you're off on an assignment, or I'm off on an assignment, and then it's the next day and we repeat it all again."

Vi squeezed her arms tighter around her chest and directed her frown at the ground, watching a pixie hurry nervously past her feet and into the tangled bushes. "I know," she said quietly. "But I'm not trying to make things worse by helping Jamon."

"I know, I understand that."

"Okay." She took a deep breath and let it out slowly. "So we both know we're not trying to make the situation worse. Why do we have to fight about it?"

"We don't. I'm sorry. This wasn't supposed to be a fight." Ryn stepped forward and pressed a brief kiss to her forehead. "We just have a lot to think about, that's all." He smiled down at her, his hand brushing her shoulder, then squeezing her upper arm. "Night, V." Then he opened a doorway in the air and vanished into it, leaving Vi wondering what the hell she was supposed to be 'thinking' about and why the ache in her chest was getting worse instead of better.

CHAPTER 2

VI DESPERATELY WANTED TO TALK TO RYN ABOUT WHATEVER was going on between them, but, as if the universe was mocking them, they were even busier than usual in the three days leading up to the Liberation Day Ball. Vi kept telling herself not to worry. If Ryn's thoughts were focused on something big-deal, like ... *don't think it, don't think it* ... an impending break-up—her heart cracked at the mere thought—he would tell her, wouldn't he? He wouldn't let her suffer for days wondering about it. Would he?

No. It was fine. They were fine. They weren't silly children anymore. They'd survived far worse than an argument over how much time they spent together, and she needed to grow up and stop worrying.

This was what she repeated to herself on Friday evening as she got ready for the ball. She didn't normally make much of an effort for these kinds of things, but given the current state of her relationship with Ryn and the message he'd sent the day before, she felt as though she had to make every effort in the world just in case ... in case ...

In case what?

Are we still going to the Lib Day Ball together? he'd asked. It was a simple message, but she couldn't get over that one word: together. As if he might go without her. As if he might go with … someone else.

Stop, she told herself in the mirror. *Stop worrying.* She blinked and returned her focus to the makeup spell for lipstick. Last year's ball, the first anniversary of their freedom from Lord Draven, was simply a great big party. This year, someone decided they should have a theme. The Council agreed, and then proceeded to come up with the dumbest theme ever: Autumn.

Raven had made a dress for Vi, following Vi's usual instructions: no puffs, frills, feathers, or dangling sleeves she might lose in her food. She'd used a shimmering orange-gold fabric and created a sleeveless dress with a sweetheart neckline that hugged the top half of Vi's body before running loosely down to her feet. Simple. Not attention-grabbing in the least. But after Ryn's message the previous day—which was followed by Vi's quick *Of course* reply—she'd hurried to Raven and Flint's house late in the evening and asked Raven to make some last-minute embellishments. She knew it was silly. If Ryn had decided to end things between the two of them, a pretty dress wasn't going to save her. She couldn't help it, though. She wanted him to see her making an effort.

She finished her makeup and stepped back to take a look at herself. Tiny crystals had been added to the top half of the dress, and the bottom half morphed into leaves—orange, maroon and gold—that shifted quietly against one another when she moved. Crystals that matched those studding the dress decorated her loose, wavy hair. Overall, it was still a simple outfit, but just a touch more special than it had been before. She could only hope Ryn noticed.

She walked downstairs, the back of the dress brushing along the floor behind her. Ryn had asked her to meet him outside her home instead of inside, which was a little strange, but she'd agreed. She didn't want to get into an argument about anything else until she was certain they'd cleared up the current argument.

Her faerie paths doorway closed, leaving her standing in the cool evening air as twilight settled around her. After checking that no one else was around, she quickly lifted the bottom of the dress and secured her stylus to the leg strap around her thigh. With that done, she rubbed her hands up and down her arms and looked around. Glow-bugs began to appear in the trees, and the quiet whisper of wings signaled an owl swooping overhead.

And that was when she noticed the strangest thing: a definite line of glow-bugs, leading away through the trees on her left. Glow-bugs didn't do that. Not naturally, anyway. They wiggled around the forest in a random fashion, never forming any particular shape. But here they were, forming a line practically from her front door.

A smile lifted her lips, and just like that, she knew everything was all right. Ryn had done this, and that meant there was no way he was angry with her. There was no way he was ending anything.

With her heart feeling lighter than it had in days, Vi followed the glow-bugs, walking beside them so her dress didn't brush over any of them. After several minutes, she reached a clearing she was familiar with. The clearing where the gargan tree used to be. *Their* gargan tree. A picnic blanket lay on the ground, cushions scattered on one side and Ryn standing on the other, his hands behind his back as he waited patiently for her.

Her smile stretched wider as she walked toward him. He said nothing, she said nothing, and when she finally stood right in front of him, he took her hand. His fingers slid between hers as she stared unceasingly into his eyes, and for a moment, only the sounds of the forest filled the air.

Eventually, she said, "I thought you were still mad at me."

"I'm sorry. You were so excited about your idea, and I shouldn't have ruined it for you."

"You didn't ruin anything. You were honest about the time we spend together. There isn't nearly enough of it, and I want that to change."

Ryn's fingers tightened around hers. "Me too."

Vi looked up and found glow-bugs floating in the air above them. "Is there an anniversary I've forgotten about?" she asked. "Aside from the anniversary of our freedom, of course."

"Yes."

Her heart stumbled over a beat or two as she tried to figure out whether he was joking or not.

"It's the anniversary of the day you remembered everything. The day you remembered how completely and utterly and—" he paused to grin "—*wildly* you love me."

Vi pressed her lips together in an attempt to smother her smile. "Well, technically that would have been last night."

Ryn shrugged. "Close enough."

Vi took another look at the picnic blanket and cushions they were standing beside. "Perhaps my memory is faulty again, but this all looks a little bit familiar. Didn't we make out in a boat filled with cushions just like these?"

"We did." Ryn looked pleased that she'd noticed.

"And this picnic blanket is actually more like a carpet. In fact, it looks a lot like a carpet we had a different make-out session on, way up in the air."

Ryn nodded. "Also correct."

With a teasing smile, Vi asked, "Will we be flying this time, or is this date staying on the ground?"

"I considered the flying carpet," Ryn said, "but it's a little difficult to balance on those things, and I wanted to make sure I didn't fall over for this part."

Vi frowned. "What part?"

"This," he said, keeping hold of her hand as he knelt down.

On one knee.

"Ohmygoodness." The words left Vi's mouth in a rush of breath as a shiver raced across her skin and her heart leaped into her throat, pounding suddenly and furiously.

"Violet Fairdale," Ryn said. "I love you more than anything and anyone, and that will never change. You've been part of my life for as long as I can remember, and for as long as I live, I want you to be at my side." His hand tightened around hers, and his lips curled into a smile. "Will you do me the incalculable honor of becoming my wife?"

Yes, her heart screamed. *Yes, yes, yes, yes, yes.* But she was so stunned, she couldn't seem to find her voice.

"I—I know we haven't really spoken about this," Ryn said, his gaze faltering just the tiniest bit. "And I know it may seem as though I've rushed into this decision, and that I'm only asking because of the argument about the amount of time we spend together, but it's something I've been thinking about for a while. I've known I wanted this since ... since before that very first kiss in the secret passage. You are the person for me. My everything. My *home*. And I know we're still very young by faerie standards, and we both work so hard that I have no idea how we'll find the time to plan a wedding, but we—"

Vi dropped to her knees and pressed her lips against his. Her hands slid around his neck and into his hair. After a second's hesitation, his arms encircled her, pulling her closer as sparks of magic danced along their skin, their tongues, their lips. The kiss was passionate, longing, filled with everything she wanted and everything she knew she could now have. She heard nothing but the joyful singing of her heart until eventually the two of them grew still and their hands found each other and their lips parted and Ryn said, "I don't think you're supposed to be kneeling."

With their foreheads touching and their hands clasped together,

Vi smiled. "I don't think you're supposed to remind me of all the reasons I should say 'no' when I'm desperately trying to say 'yes.'"

Ryn leaned back so he could properly meet her gaze. "Yes?"

She couldn't believe there was still a question in his voice. Could he really have any doubt after that kiss? Her hands moved away from his and reached up to frame his face. "Yes. With all my heart."

THE ARTIST

This story is Chase's point of view of the first time he and Calla met. Read it any time after *A Faerie's Secret*, Creepy Hollow Book Four.

CHAPTER 1

CHASE TUGGED HIS JACKET OFF AS HE STRODE ALONG THE Underground tunnel into Sivvyn Quarter. He hadn't used the tunnels in a while, but a broken stylus meant no access to the faerie paths. It had been careless of him to let the young Lord Farrowtongue close enough to get hold of his stylus. The man had turned out to be stronger than most, which had taken Chase by surprise.

This conflict between Farrowtongue and his cousin needed to end before anyone else got hurt. The two young men were already responsible for the death of a dwarf family that had been caught in the fire at the base of the Bordeon Mountains. It was a miracle the Guild wasn't involved yet.

Chase reached his door, swung the jacket over one shoulder, and bent slightly as he traced a forefinger over the keyhole, drawing the unlocking pattern. He muttered the spell that went along with it, then straightened as the keyhole glowed for a moment. The lock clicked. He opened the door and walked into his living room—and froze.

A girl stood there, on the other side of the room near the desk, streaks of brilliant gold in her hair, and eyes just as bright. Chase's hand tightened on the jacket as he fought the instinct to attack first and ask questions later. A stupid decision, perhaps, since this girl might be a far bigger threat than she looked. Especially when he had the unnerving feeling that he recognized her.

"Who are you?" he asked.

"I'm …" She hesitated too long, and he knew she was concocting a lie. "An admirer of your art," she finished.

Well, that might be true, but it certainly wasn't the whole truth. "I see." He watched the rising panic in her eyes as he slowly closed the door behind him. It wasn't a look he enjoyed seeing. It reminded him too much of—

Stop. No need to dredge up the past.

It wasn't a look he enjoyed seeing, but he didn't want her trying to run past him to get away. He needed answers. He needed to know who she was and why she was here, in a home that only Gaius and Elizabeth should know about.

He stepped forward and draped the jacket over the back of an armchair, taking his time, allowing tension to build, hoping that with every passing second she'd grow closer to blurting out answers. She said nothing, though, and it seemed her focus had shifted elsewhere. His arms? His tattoos?

"Why do you look familiar?" he asked, hoping to startle her into giving up the truth.

Her gaze snapped back to his. "Familiar?" She started laughing then—*laughing*, of all things. "Have you met many gold faeries?"

"No. I haven't." He saw her fingers twitch then. Preparing to reach for a weapon? She wouldn't be fast enough. No one was ever fast enough. "How did you get in here?" he asked. "The door has some powerful protection on it."

A cocky look appeared in her eyes. "I guess I'm just that good."

He almost laughed at that. Almost. "Just that good, huh? I doubt it. You're a faerie, which means the most likely way you got in here is through the faerie paths. But this home has no name or number for you to whisper to the paths, and I've taken great care to make sure there are only two other people who know what the inside of it looks like. So how did you get in?"

Her arrogance didn't waver. "You might want to block your keyhole."

"It is blocked. No magic can get through it."

"Well, I guess you forgot about light." Without pause, she threw her arm up, no doubt raising a shield between the two of them. With one hand, she yanked a stylus from her boot, and in her other hand—

Chase allowed himself only a split second to be surprised by what he saw in her hand. It was the bangle. The bronze bangle with the shimmering green gems and the clockwork parts. Was that the reason she was here? Had she somehow heard of the magic contained within this jewelry?

He swept a hand through the air, releasing the power that was always there, rippling beneath the surface of his control. It broke through her shield easily, knocking her backward into the desk chair. As she slid to the floor, he crossed the room to retrieve the bangle. She raised her free hand, something flashed and sparkled in the air, and a second later a glittering metal star spun toward him. He dodged, and the weapon nicked his arm as it flew past.

So that's what she is, he realized as she vaulted over the couch and ran for the door. "Not only an *art admirer,*" he said as he turned to find her twisting the handle uselessly, "but a guardian and a thief as well."

She spun back to face him, her brow furrowing in concentration. She was probably drawing more power, hoping to—

Talons ripped into his front door, tearing the entire things off its hinges. A wild roar erupted from the other side before the door was flung sideways, knocking the girl to the floor as a dragon shoved its snarling head into Chase's home.

CHAPTER 2

THERE WAS NO TIME FOR CHASE TO FIGURE OUT HOW THE hell a *dragon* had found its way into the Underground tunnels. It lumbered into his living room, breathing scorching flames and increasing rapidly in size. He flattened himself against a wall as the beast's enormous body filled the room and crushed the burning furniture. With his hand raised, he released wave upon wave of power, but it made no difference to the dragon.

Impossible, he thought, a hint of fear pricking at him for the first time in … in years, possibly. He ignored the searing heat and continued his meaningless assault on the dragon as he edged his way around the room, closer to the splintered door and the fallen girl. She wasn't moving. If he could just get to her before the flames engulfed the entire—

And then it was all gone. The dragon, the flames, the heat, the damage. The girl. He swung around, but everything was in its place, just as it had been the moment before the dragon ripped through the door.

The dragon that was never here, he realized.

Chase took a moment to marvel at that fact. To wonder at the kind of magic that could construct an illusion so complex. Was the girl an illusion too? No. The bangle was gone, he noted, so she had definitely been here. But how had she found the power to cast a spell that complex in so short a time?

Unless … unless it wasn't a spell. Unless it was a Griffin Ability. Chase glanced at the tiny ship floating on enchanted stormy waters within the bottle on his desk. *How daring of her*, he thought. *How very, very daring.* Working for the Guild while hiding a Griffin Ability. What would they do to her if they found out?

What the Guild might do wasn't important at this moment, though. Getting the bangle back was Chase's priority. He removed a small round mirror from his jacket pocket. Which member of his team should he start with? Lumethon, probably. She controlled the Underground lizard network. Those tiny creatures never missed anything. If the girl was somewhere Underground, they'd find her.

He tapped the mirror and spoke her name to it. When the haziness faded and Lumethon's face appeared within the glossy surface, Chase didn't waste time with greetings. "A faerie girl just stole the bangle," he said. "She's easy to spot. Gold hair and eyes. If you find her anywhere Underground, let me know."

"Sure thing."

Chase swiped a finger across the mirror's surface, then spoke a second name: "Gaius." Gaius kept the tracking owls at the mountain, but they could be sent here fairly quickly. If any imprint of the girl's magic remained in this room by the time the owls got here, they'd easily pick it up. And they'd easily track her down.

Before Gaius could answer the call, though, a message from Lumethon appeared on Chase's amber.

Easy peasy. She's in Club Deviant.

Club Deviant? What was the silly girl doing there?

Chase strode across the room to his desk, retrieved a spare stylus from the bottom drawer, and opened a doorway to the faerie paths.

Seconds later, he walked into the smoky haze of Club Deviant. It wasn't all that busy, and he easily spotted the gold-haired girl sitting at the bar. He walked between the dancers, slid onto the stool beside her, and asked, "Do you have a death wish?" She pulled back, her eyes widening as she recognized him. "What are you doing in a club owned by the number one guardian hater in Creepy Hollow?"

She hesitated, and it occurred to him that she might not know who owned this bar. "What do you—Wait." She shook her head. "How did you find me?"

"Word travels quickly when silly young guardians decide to risk their lives Underground."

"I'm not a silly—"

"No, you're a thief."

Her eyebrows pulled together, a crease forming between them. "*I'm* a thief? You're the one who stole the bangle in the first place." She raised her arm and waved it in front him. "I'll be returning this to the Guild, and there's nothing you can do to—"

"You *put it on?*" The stool almost fell over as he slid backward off it, hastily putting some distance between him and the girl. "What the hell is wrong with you?" *Be calm*, he reminded himself. *Don't freak her out. Don't let her trigger it.*

"There's nothing wrong with me," the girl said as she stood. Clearly she had no idea what this bangle could do. Had the Guild instructed her to retrieve it without giving her any details? Or had she simply found it by accident? "And since this club is apparently owned by someone with an intense hatred for guardians," she added, "I think I should go."

"Wait." He stepped closer, then dodged as she sent sparks flying his way. He raised his hands. "Just give me the bangle and I'll let you go."

"*You'll* let *me* go?" she repeated. "Have you forgotten the dragon already?"

Damn, this girl had guts. He wondered how she'd react if she knew exactly who it was she was speaking to. "Have you forgotten the power that knocked out your shield in an instant and swept you to the ground?" he countered.

She hesitated a moment too long, the confidence in her gaze wavering just the slightest. But then she shrugged and said, "That was hardly power. Why don't we have a second go, and you can show me if you've got any power left after—"

"This isn't a game, little guardian." He closed the distance between them and grabbed her arm—the arm without the dangerous jewelry. "Someone is coming for that bangle, and you don't want to be here when he arrives." Chase didn't know for certain that Saber was on his way, but he knew it wouldn't be long before he showed up. He also had eyes everywhere, looking out for his stolen power.

The girl tried to wrench her arm away, but Chase wasn't planning on letting go without getting the bangle first. "If you want it so badly, *old man*," she said through gritted teeth, "then why haven't you taken it already?"

Old man? He ignored the weak insult and leaned closer as he answered, "Because, silly girl, I'd have to cut off your arm."

He was hoping the truth would scare her, and it seemed he was right. After a pause, she said, "Fine. You can have it." With her right hand, she slid the bangle off her left arm. She held it up between them.

Chase released his grip on her and reached for the bangle. "Thank you."

She smiled at him—and then she hurled it over his shoulder.

With an angry cry, he spun around and dashed after the bangle. He couldn't see where it had landed, but he had to get hold of it before anyone else did. It must have hit the wall and bounced back somewhere. He searched the floor. He searched between the dancers. And then he realized …

She'd done it again. Dammit! Another trick. Another illusion. He looked back, expecting to find an empty stool where he'd last seen the girl. The stool was indeed empty, but behind the bar, where a door led to a passage he'd never been down, he saw her. Being dragged away by the elves who worked for the club owner.

Chase cursed and took off after her. A drakoni and another elf tried to stop him, but he dealt with them quickly. A few well-aimed kicks and punches, plus a bit of stunner magic thrown in, and they wouldn't be getting up for a while. He sensed it then, the vibration in the air that meant the bangle's magic was about to be released.

He dashed around the bar and into the passageway. He could see the girl at the other end, in a room where the elves stood guard. The air rippled past him, more noticeable this time. "TAKE IT OFF!" he yelled.

She looked back at him, her gaze landing on his as the vibration intensified. He ran faster—but it was too late.

She was gone.

I LOVE YOU, YOU IDIOT

This is the story of Gemma and Perry, two side characters from Calla's part of the Creepy Hollow series. It's the story of how they figured out their feelings for one another.
Yes, it's another story about a kiss.

Read this any time after *A Faerie's Curse*,
Creepy Hollow Book Six.

CHAPTER 1

First Year

FOUR HOURS INTO DAY ONE OF GUARDIAN TRAINING, AND
Gemma Alcourt had made a grand total of zero friends. Not exactly
encouraging for someone who'd planned to be far more popular at
the Guild than she'd been in junior school. There, most of the faerie
children had teased her for being a halfling—which she wasn't;
black and brown were two completely different colors and her hair
consisted of *both*, so she was *all* faerie, thank you very much—but
Gemma was certain her classmates at the Guild wouldn't bother
with childish taunts like that. She would impress her peers with her
knowledge of the Creepy Hollow Guild, and she'd wind up popular
in no time.

Sadly, things hadn't gone down that way. No one cared that
she'd been inside the Guild dozens of times before, that she knew
where everything was, or that she easily led her team to victory
during the orientation treasure hunt this morning. Oh no. Having
insider knowledge of the Guild didn't matter. The only thing that
seemed to matter was guardian heritage—and Gemma was sorely
lacking in that department. Her mom was an admin at the Guild,

135

and her dad was a florist—the furthest thing from cool, according to Saskia Starkweather, loudest mouth in the class. Saskia's grand-mother was Head Councilor of the Guild of Guardians years ago, so of course that gave Saskia more bragging rights than anyone else.

So that was how Gemma found herself sitting alone—*alone!*—in the dining hall during lunch. Ugh. This was even worse than junior school. At least there she'd had Cami. But Cami planned to be a teacher one day, not a guardian, so Gemma was left to face Guild training—and eating lunch, it seemed—on her own. Well, not entirely on her own, if you considered the four girls sitting at the other end of the table. But they were several years older than Gemma and hadn't looked in her direction once, so she didn't think they counted.

Thwack.

She sucked in a breath and jerked backward as something light-weight smacked her forehead. It dropped onto her sandwich before coming to rest beside her tray.

A crumpled-up wad of paper.

Gemma's cheeks burned as her eyes flashed up and around the dining hall. There—one of her classmates, whipping his gaze away from her and laughing into his glass. She stood before she could think about it, swiping the crumpled paper from the table as she went. It was the tall boy, the one with green in his eyes and hair. He'd answered every question in their first lesson with some silly nonsense answer until Saskia turned on him and told him to shut up. Gemma marched between the tables and benches and stopped in front of him. "Trying to get my attention?" she demanded, holding out the scrunched paper.

The tall boy looked up, his eyes widening at the sight of her standing right there. The shorter, broader boy sitting beside him turned red and focused his gaze firmly on his tray. *Good*, Gemma thought. *At least one of them's embarrassed.*

"Yes, actually," the tall boy answered. "If you open that bit of paper, you'll find an invitation to join us here at our table."

"Right. Sure I will."

"You're Gemma, right?" He nodded to the red-faced boy. "This is Ned. I'm Perry."

Gemma's frown deepened. She'd seen the complete list of names on her mother's desk weeks before training began, and there'd been no Perry. But there had been a— "Peregrine," she said. "That's your name."

The boy made a great show of shuddering. "Okay. I think we're even now."

"Even?"

"How about I never throw anything at you ever again, and you never call me Peregrine?"

Gemma simply glared at him, not willing to give in so easily while humiliation still burned her face.

"And you can sit with us," Peregrine added.

Gemma's hand tightened around the ball of paper. "What makes you think I want to sit with you?"

He shrugged. "Maybe the longing gaze you were giving those fifth-year girls at the other end of your table."

Gemma threw the wad of paper square in Peregrine's face and flounced away. *Idiot.* She'd rather sit alone than with someone like him. She dropped into her seat just as something hit the edge of her tray: the offending ball of paper, less crumpled this time, a word visible near the creased edge of the paper.

... us.

Reluctantly, Gemma nudged the crinkles apart until all the words became visible:

Hey, come sit with us.

CHAPTER 2

Fifth Year

"Yeeha!" Perry crowed from the classroom doorway. "We are so gonna dominate this year." He weaved between the desks and dropped into the chair in front of Gemma. At the front of the classroom, Saskia muttered something unpleasant as she removed her textbooks from her bag. She didn't appreciate people not taking lessons or training seriously—which was pretty much all the time where Perry was concerned.

"What was that, Sas?" Perry asked, draping his lanky frame across the chair and leaning sideways as if he hadn't a care in the world. "Stick still up your butt? What a shame. It must be getting pretty uncomfortable after four years. Or has it been there your entire life?"

Saskia turned to face him and, with utter calm, said, "I will stab you in the face, *Peregrine*."

And the thing about Saskia was that she probably would. With precision and skill. And then she'd ask how many points she earned for it afterward. Gemma often wondered if Saskia sat on the topmost rung of the popularity ladder because people actually liked her or because no one dared attempt to knock her off. Except for Perry, of course, and sometimes Gemma when she felt particularly brave or fed up. But Perry and Gemma were right at the bottom of that ladder, and any shots fired barely reached Saskia.

"Just drop it," Gemma said quietly, reaching forward and squeezing Perry's shoulder. "No need for you to get stabbed in the face over something as silly as the stick wedged permanently up Saskia's backside."

"True. It would be a shame to mess up a face this good-looking."

"Uh huh." Gemma rolled her eyes as Ned walked through the door. He kept his gaze down as he navigated his way toward the empty desk next to Perry. He may have warmed up to Gemma over time, but he still found most of the female population intimidating.

"Happy final year," he said as he lowered his bag and sat down. "Not much longer to go, and we can leave this place behind."

"Ah, come on," Perry said, slapping Ned playfully on the back. "You know you want to work here for the rest of your life."

Ned snorted. "No thanks. I'm looking forward to working as a guardian, but I won't be doing it here."

Another few trainees walked into the classroom, followed by Irwin, one of the mentors. Gemma checked the time on her amber, which told her there were still another few minutes before class was scheduled to begin. Irwin placed a textbook and scroll on the table at the front. The textbook flipped open to a page near the beginning of the book while Irwin sat, unrolled the scroll, and leaned back to read it.

"Oh, hey, guess what," Gemma said, leaning forward and tapping Perry's shoulder as she remembered the conversation she'd had with her mom the night before. "Someone new is joining our class."

"What?" He swiveled to face her. "But it's fifth year. No one ever joins this late."

"Must be a transfer trainee from another Guild," Ned said.

"Nope." Gemma shook her head. "It's Ryn Larkenwood's younger sister. She's never been a trainee at any Guild before, but she's had private training and written a whole bunch of exams, so I guess the Guild thinks she's good enough."

"Did her brother train her?" Perry asked.

"I don't know."

"If he did, she must be good." He grinned. "Saskia's gonna hate her. This is awesome."

"Perry!" Gemma hissed. "Don't be an insensitive brute."

"Brute?" Perry laughed. "You know I was joking. Obviously I'll be super welcoming and friendly and *not* sit back to watch the entertainment. Unless this new girl is just as much of a troll as Saskia. Then I will definitely be getting front-row tickets to the showdown."

Gemma slid down a little and kicked Perry's chair.

He shook his head. "So mature, Miss Alcourt. So mature."

"Only as mature as you, Mr. Foundland."

Ned sighed and faced forward. "Another year of this."

"Well, guys," Irwin said, standing and placing his hands on his hips, "this is it. The last time you get the first-day-of-the-year speech." Gemma looked around as Irwin launched into the 'start strong, finish strong' motivational stuff. Had the new girl somehow slipped in without anyone noticing? No. All Gemma saw were familiar faces. She focused on Irwin again as he finished off his 'speech' by reminding everyone that this year would be their busiest year yet, with no time for fooling around if they all hoped to pass. His gaze lingered on Perry for a moment before he clapped his hands together and said, "Well then, let's begin with some history." Several people groaned and slumped further down in their seats. "Oh, and one more thing," Irwin added. "A new trainee will be joining your class today. She hasn't been in a Guild environment before, so I trust you'll all show her around and make her feel welcome."

Silence greeted his words before Saskia said, "Is this some kind of welcome-to-fifth-year joke?"

Irwin frowned. "Why would I be joking?"

"Because people don't join in fifth year," Saskia said. "They don't even join in fourth year. They start at the beginning or they don't start at all."

"Yeah, remember when Saskia's cousin wanted to join the Guild when he was fifteen and they wouldn't let him?" Blaze piped up.

"Saskia knows why her cousin didn't get in," Irwin said, "and it had nothing to do with the fact that he was older than a first-year trainee." He looked around the room. "The Council has decided that Miss Larkenwood's abilities are up to fifth-year standard, and I don't think any of you are in a position to question the Council's decisions."

"Larkenwood?" Saskia muttered under her breath. "Now we know how she got in."

Irwin frowned at her before moving his gaze across the rest of the class again. "I'd like you to welcome Miss Larkenwood and make her transition into Guild life as easy as possible, understood?"

Gemma looked around to see if anyone was nodding, but most of her classmates stared down at their desks.

"Wonderful," Irwin said, clearly interpreting the silence as compliance. He turned to his open textbook. "We're going to start off the year by taking a more in-depth look at ..." He trailed off as the door slowly swung open. "Ah," Irwin said as Gemma leaned to the side to get a better look past Perry. "Here she is."

CHAPTER 3

For the first time since junior school, Gemma had a friend who was a girl. Finally! She now had someone to talk girl stuff with. Stuff like that edible nail polish she'd seen recently, and the crush she had on Rick the Seer trainee, and her super embarrassing secret: the one about never having been kissed before. No way could she mention things like that to Perry or Ned. Ned would turn red and exit the conversation as quickly as possible, and Perry would simply laugh at her. Then he'd probably ask if he could taste the edible nail polish.

So Gemma was immensely grateful for Calla Larkenwoods's arrival. Sure, Calla was guarded and quiet, but that was because of her crazy assumption that Gemma, Perry and Ned would soon wind up afraid of her. And it was true that the stories about her making other people crazy were a bit scary, but Gemma didn't believe them. No one on the Council would have let Calla into the Guild if they could sense Unseelie magic in her.

But there were plenty of people who *weren't* happy Calla was here. Like her mentor Olive. Olive was the reason Calla was currently recovering on a mat on one side of the training center. The vindictive woman had forced Calla to do the same obstacle course over and over and *over* until she deemed Calla's performance good enough. Then she'd left the training center looking completely bored.

With the aid of her magic, Gemma helped Perry and Ned move all the obstacles back against the wall while Calla caught her breath. She sat up just as they finished. "Hey, thanks," she said, looking around at the cleared obstacles. She pushed herself up onto shaky legs. "You didn't need to do that."

"I think we did," Gemma said. "Looks like you need all your magic just to keep your legs working."

"Do you think you'll have recovered by tonight?" Perry asked.

"Yes, probably. Why, do you have something exciting planned?"

"Well, *we* don't," Perry said, a grin appearing on his face, "but someone else does, and we've been invited. Sort of. I mean, I *found* an invite."

"So … we're actually *not* invited?" Calla asked with a frown.

Gemma opened her mouth to explain, but Perry got there first. "It was this follow-the-clue-and-find-an-invite sort of thing. I saw it written on someone's leg when we were Underground last week looking for you. So I followed the clue. And now we have an invitation."

"Is this an Underground party?" she asked.

"No, it's at the top of Estellyn Tower."

"Seriously?" Calla looked from Perry to Gemma, and Gemma nodded, her smile growing wider. "That place is *super* fancy," Calla added, which Gemma was already aware of. It was one of the reasons she was so excited to attend this party. "Are you sure we're allowed to go?"

"Well, we have three entirely legitimate invitations," Perry said, "so yeah."

"I'm not going," Ned added quickly, his gaze barely meeting Calla's before flicking away. "So the third invitation is yours."

"The clue led to this random old tree," Perry explained, "and when I put my hand inside one of the knots, I was able to pull out an invitation. Only one per person, though, so I got Gemma and Ned to go back with me so we could get another two."

"Because we can't let him have all the fun at a celebrity party on his own," Gemma added, bouncing a little on her toes. "We need to keep an eye on him. So can you come?"

"I doubt I'll ever get another chance to mix with the elite fae upper class," Calla said, "so yes. Definitely."

"Awesome!" Gemma looped her arm through Calla's as they headed for the training center door. "Now what are we going to *wear*?"

CHAPTER 4

PERRY PICTURED THE INSIDE OF GEMMA'S HOUSE AS HE waited in the shadows outside, leaning against a tree. Her home always looked a little bit as though an enchanted tornado had just rushed through. It sounded like tonight was no different. Through the tree trunk and the glamour—which wasn't as high quality as the glamour Perry's parents had on their home—Perry could hear Gemma's two younger brothers laughing and shouting. And then Gemma's older sister Jazz shouting at them. Jazz didn't officially live at home anymore, but she didn't particularly like the house she now shared with two of her friends who'd also recently graduated, so she spent at least half her time back at home.

A portion of the tree trunk shimmered and light spilled out of the doorway that appeared. "Quickly," Jazz whispered. She was a dark shape against the bright light, but Perry knew it was her.

"I know, I know. Stupid shoe ..." A second silhouette—Gemma—stumbled toward the doorway. "You'll keep Mom and Dad away from my room, right?"

"Obviously. And don't make a noise when you get back."

"Of course I won't make a noise."

"And don't take spells from strangers."

"Oh my goodness, Jazz, I'm not five years old."

"Okay, okay. Just hurry up and leave. Mom and Dad are gonna be back downstairs any second."

"Right, sorry." Gemma stepped outside, and the doorway sealed up behind her. "Perry?" she called.

"Yeah, I'm here." He pushed away from the tree and walked toward her, igniting a ball of light above his hand as he went. The light spread, illuminating the space between him and—

Perry stopped. He stared. Was that really *Gemma* standing in front of him? It didn't look anything like her. How did her hair get so straight and shiny? And how did her eyes become so striking, and her lips so ... full? And *damn*, that dress was like a second skin. She even had ... Perry's face warmed as his gaze snapped away from the swell of her chest.

"Perry? Hello?" Gemma waved a hand in front of his face.

He blinked. "What?"

"Who's directing the paths? You or me?"

"Uh, I'll do it." He turned back to the tree he'd been leaning against, shaking his head a little. He wrote across the bark with his stylus and opened a way to the faerie paths, instructing himself to *focus* and stop thinking of the pretty girl standing right behind him.

About half an hour later, Perry, Gemma and Calla had successfully made their way to the topmost level of Estellyn Tower and into the midst of designer Lucien de la Mer's party. Though packed with faeries mingling and chatting, and others swaying and twisting in time to the music, it was nothing like the Underground clubs Perry occasionally hung out at. Those clubs were smoky and dirty and he could barely hear himself think over the pounding beat. But this place ... this place oozed sophistication. Good thing Perry had dug through to the back of his wardrobe for that suit his mother forced him to get for last year's Lib Day Ball.

After weaving through the dancers and each taking a different drink from one of the floating trays, the three of them ended up near the floor-to-ceiling windows that cycled through images of exotic locations from around the world. "Do you think he's here?" Gemma asked as she looked around. "Lucien, I mean. Or do you think he's hiding somewhere in one of his other rooms, relaxing in a bathrobe while all these people party it up at his expense."

"Well, I have no idea what he looks like, so I won't know if I see him," Calla said. She raised her glass to her lips and took a sip. "Mm. Tastes like sunrise."

"Sunrises don't have a taste, silly." Gemma eyed the floating jelly spheres in her colorless drink with a frown.

"But if they did, they'd taste like this."

Perry sipped his drink and almost spat it back out. It reminded him of that horrid tonic is mother had made him drink every morning before breakfast as a child. "Mine tastes like medicine," he said, screwing his face up. As one of the trays floated by, he placed his half-finished drink on it.

Gemma's mouth dropped open. "Perry, you can't put it back!"

"I just did. Come on, dance with me," he said to Gemma as a lively beat wove its way through the party. He kept getting the crazy urge to move closer to her, and dancing was probably the safest way to do that without her thinking something was wrong with him.

"Oh. Um ..." Gemma looked at Calla. "But what about—"

"I'll be fine," Calla said. "You guys dance. I'll find you later."

Perry took Gemma's hand, just as he did whenever they traveled through the faerie paths together. *This is no different*, he told himself, despite the fact that he was more aware of the nerve endings in his hand than ever before. He tugged her onto the dance floor, wiggling his hips in an exaggerated manner. "Oh my gosh, *stop*," Gemma said, but she was laughing so he kept going. She joined in, though she was far less wild and far more self-conscious. She kept looking around, which Perry didn't mind; it gave him the chance to examine her more closely without her realizing he was staring. She really was pretty tonight. Not that he thought she was *ugly* on a normal day. He'd just ... never considered it before.

When the music slowed to something more sensual and a woman nearby started sliding her body up and down against her partner's as she swayed to the beat, Perry panicked. He and Gemma were friends, and things would get awkward very quickly if they started dancing together to this kind of music. He didn't *want* to dance with Gemma like that. Right? Right. It would be super weird. His instincts kicked in, telling him it was about time to joke about something, like the bazillion piercings the musicians in the band were wearing, or the flapping, feathery backside of that dress over there, which made the unfortunate wearer's butt look like—

"Hey, let's try some of the food," Gemma said, pushing him toward a passing tray. "I bet it's amazing."

"Yeah, okay." After tasting that medicine-like drink, Perry wasn't sure he agreed with her on the 'amazing' part, but he was happy to move away from the dancers. He let Gemma steer him toward the tray she had her eye on.

"But you can't put something back if you don't like it," she added.

"Where must I put it then? On a chair? Down the back of someone's dress?"

"No!"

"I'll give it to you then."

"Fine." They reached the tray, and Gemma took a white cube covered in tiny specks of brightly colored candy. It was small enough for her to eat in one bite. Perry looked away from her lips —they were just *lips*, for goodness' sake—and took a miniature golden apple. It tasted a thousand times better than his drink. "So good," Gemma said when she'd finished chewing. "I want to taste everything."

It became a game then, hunting down the floating trays and trying something new from each one. As time passed, Gemma giggled more and became less inhibited until eventually she'd abandoned the food game entirely in favor of dancing through the crowd, waving her arms around. "Hey, Gemma?" Perry said, keeping close to her. "Are you okay?"

"Uh huh." She whipped her head from side to side, her hair swinging out around her. "Dance with me, Perry!"

"Uh …" He wanted to, but something wasn't right. "Maybe we should get a drink. Some water," he corrected.

"Don't be so boring, Peregrine." She twirled around and around, her arms in the air above her head. "Ugh, I wish he had come, you know? I told him to get an invitation. I told him where to go. But he said he couldn't."

Perry reached for one of her arms and stopped her spinning before she knocked into someone. "I don't know who you're talking about, Gem."

"You know." She wobbled closer to him and took his face in both her hands. "You must know him," she said, her eyes wide but somehow looking through him. "Everyone knows him."

Her touch sent his heart galloping, but it was so uncharacteristic of Gemma that it made him uncomfortable. He gently removed her hands from his face. "You ate something strange, didn't you."

"I ate something *amazing*," she corrected. "Lots of amazings. Amaze … ing." She started giggling again and leaned against him. He held her upright before she could slide onto the floor.

"Need to find Calla," he muttered to himself.

It took some time because of the number of people he had to push past and because Gemma kept getting distracted by a shiny hair ornament or a friendly person or another exotic delicacy. In the end, it was Gemma who saw Calla first. "Callaaa! There you are!" Gemma stumbled away from Perry and flung her arms around Calla.

"Hey, we've been looking for you for a while," Perry said. "I think—"

"Oh my *gosh*," Gemma said, hanging onto Calla's arm and staring wide-eyed at the guy standing next to her. "You're the hot tattoo guy."

Hot tattoo guy? Something lurched uncomfortably in the region of Perry's stomach. This was the guy he and Gemma had found Calla with Underground last week. Was he also the guy Gemma had been talking about earlier?

"And you're standing *right here*," Gemma continued, still staring at the tattoo artist. "Know what? I've always wanted to get a tattoo on—" she giggled, then whispered "—*my butt*. Do you do butt tattoos? Please say yes. You're the *best* tattoo artist in the whole world."

Her butt. She just had to mention her butt. Which Perry had, of course, never thought about before. Until tonight when he noticed how perfect it looked in that slinky dress she—

He pushed the thought from his mind as he realized Calla was looking at him. "I think she ate something weird," he said quickly. "She's been like this for the past ten minutes or so."

"Some of the chocolate bonbons have alcohol inside them," the tattoo artist said. "Human alcohol, not faerie alcohol. It acts quickly on our systems."

"That's probably it," Perry said grudgingly. Of course that was it. He should have realized without having to be told by the 'hot tattoo guy.' "She ate a whole load of different bonbons."

"They were AH-mazing," Gemma said loudly.

"I'm sure they were," Calla said, patting Gemma's arm. "Perry, maybe you should—" She ducked as a group of sprites flying in formation swooped over her head.

"This Lucien de la Mer guy provides the strangest entertainment," the tattoo artist commented.

"Um, I don't feel so good," Gemma said with a frown. She bent over and leaned on her knees, breathing in deeply.

Perry rubbed her arm. "It'll pass soon," he said as soothingly as possible. "Let's get you home, okay?" He looked up and found an unfamiliar woman speaking in low tones to the tattoo artist.

"… not sticking around to find out," she said. "I'm leaving. I can't afford to get caught here if things go south and security locks this place down."

Well that didn't sound good. "Calla, we should really get Gemma home," Perry said.

Seeming distracted, Calla pulled her concerned gaze away from the tattoo artist and back to Perry. "Yes. Can you take her? I need to help Chase with something here."

"Uh, okay." Perry frowned. He should probably ask what was going on, but his attention snapped back to Gemma as she made a retching sound. "I'll message Gemma's sister," he added quickly. "She helped her sneak out, so hopefully she's still around to distract the parents while I sneak her back in." He took Gemma's arm and draped it across his shoulders before heading into the crowd of people. By the time they'd reached the elevator on the other side of the enormous room, Gemma was moaning.

"If I throw up … on your suit … I'm sorry."

"You'd better not," he joked as he pulled her into the elevator. "This is my best suit. And by best, I mean *only*."

Gemma managed to last until they'd made it out of Estellyn Tower, into the faerie paths, and out the other side near her home before being sick. Perry stepped out of the way just in time and pulled her hair back. "So … embarrassing," she moaned when her body had finished heaving.

"Don't worry about it," Perry said as a doorway opened and Jazz hurried out. He wanted to tell Gemma she was still pretty, even when she was throwing up, but Jazz was right there, taking Gemma's arm. Besides, there wasn't really a way to say something like that without sounding totally weird.

CHAPTER 5

NED'S FIST SWUNG STRAIGHT AT PERRY'S FACE. PERRY DODGED —at least, he thought he dodged. He'd certainly planned to, but somehow he found himself on his back on the mat with blinding pain flashing across the left side of his jaw. He groaned and squinted through half-open eyelids. Ned looked down at him, hands on his hips, barely breathless. "What's up with you?" he asked. "It's like you're not even trying."

Perry sat up, moving his jaw from side to side to check it still worked. The pain slowly began to subside. "I'm a little distracted, remember?" His brows drew together as he looked across the training center. Everyone was going about their morning sessions as if nothing was wrong. As if one of their classmates hadn't been abducted from within the Guild yesterday.

Ned extended his hand to Perry and pulled him up. "I'm sure Calla's fine," he said quietly. "Someone brought her back here last night, so if she's still in the healing wing this morning, that means she's recovering."

"Yeah," Perry muttered. Ned was probably right, but it was still scary that some unauthorized person had managed to get into the healing wing and take both Calla and her mother. Why would someone do that? Did it have something to do with the strange stories that always seemed to follow Calla around? Did it have something to do with … what he'd seen at the party?

The party …

Perry's mind turned to the other person who kept distracting his thoughts: Gemma. She'd missed school yesterday after the party at Estellyn Tower, and this morning she'd already finished breakfast by the time he and Ned got to the dining hall. "I'm gonna see what I can find out about Calla," she'd told them before hurrying away. Perry wondered if she felt awkward about her drunken state, or if she was just in a rush to find out what had happened to—

"Hello?" Ned said loudly. "Are we going again? This session isn't over yet. You still have a chance to kick my ass."

Right, like that was going to happen. Even on Perry's best days, Ned was better at hand-to-hand. Now, with two girls taking up the space inside his head, Perry didn't stand a chance.

"Hey, guys." Perry looked past Ned and saw Gemma hurrying toward them. He reminded himself to act normal. After all, nothing had changed. He'd simply noticed for the first time that Gemma was attractive, but that didn't mean things had to be different now.

"Did you see her?" he asked as Gemma reached them. "Is she okay?"

"Yeah." Gemma dropped her bag onto the floor beside the mat.

"Did she tell you what happened?"

"Not really. She said some men came for her mother. Calla was in the room at the time, so they took her too. Apparently she isn't allowed to tell us any more than that."

"How odd," Perry said. "Why would anyone want her mother?"

"Someone broke into Calla's home, remember?" Gemma said, her eyebrows raised. "And then after they moved house, someone broke in again and attacked both her parents. That's why her mom was in the healing wing in the first place. So yesterday's abduction must be related to those attacks."

"Right. Of course." Perry needed to get his head screwed back on properly. He'd make a terrible guardian one day if he kept forgetting important details like this. "But that still doesn't tell us *why* someone's targeting Calla's parents," he added, hoping to redeem himself. "And maybe it's something to do with Calla, not her mom or her dad."

"Why do you say that?" Gemma asked with a frown. "Because of all the stories about her? You know those have been embellished by people like Saskia. Calla definitely isn't Unseelie. We'd be able to feel it if her magic was different. Right?" She looked at Ned.

He nodded. "We're always being told there's something different about Unseelie magic. We're supposed to be able to sense it. I think they should expose us to it during our training. How are we supposed to know what it feels like otherwise?"

Gemma rolled her eyes. "Sure, let's ask the Guild to arrange a field trip to the Unseelie Court. I'm sure that would work out well."

"Look, I need to tell you guys something," Perry said. He looked at Gemma. "After I took you home from the party the other night, I went back. I knew Calla was still there, and I didn't want to leave her alone with that guy. I had just got out of the elevator and I was looking around for Calla, and then she just … appeared. Literally. Out of thin air. Not walking out of the faerie paths, but just … mid-conversation with that tattoo artist, the two of them just appeared."

"That is weird," Gemma said. "Did anyone else see?"

"No one seemed to notice."

"What are you saying?" Ned asked. "Some of the stories might be true?"

"But those stories are all about her making weird stuff happen to other people," Gemma said. "Appearing out of nothing is different."

"Yeah, but it's still something we shouldn't be able to do," Ned said. "If she's playing around with abnormal spells, we need to tell someone before she gets herself hurt or gets us into trouble."

"She's not going to get us into trouble, Ned," Gemma said. "She just—"

"Miss Alcourt." The mentor on duty, Anise, walked up to the three of them. "How nice of you to join us. I assume you have a reason for being absent for most of the first session?"

"Uh …"

"And I assume there's an equally important reason that the two of you—" she looked at Perry and Ned "—have stopped sparring despite the fact that we still have fifteen minutes left of this session?"

"Yes, it's the most *awful* story," Perry said, getting ready to embellish the heck out of Calla's situation. "Calla was simply minding her own business and visiting her poor mother, when this brute of a—"

"I'm already aware of that story, Mr. Foundland," Anise said. "Please get on with your training."

CHAPTER 6

GEMMA FELT TERRIBLE SPYING ON HER NEW FRIEND, BUT IF Calla was using dangerous spells, then Gemma thought it was something she should know about. Perry suggested they just come out and ask her about it, and Gemma agreed that was the right thing to do. But then Calla had turned all distant and moody right after her brother's wedding, and since then she always seemed to be training or studying or on another assignment. So now Gemma and Perry were spying on her—*observing*, Perry called it—whenever they got the chance. Ned didn't join them. He didn't actually know about the 'observing.' He wouldn't approve.

At the moment, their observation was taking place in the library. Gemma had asked Calla if she wanted to hang out that afternoon, and Calla said she needed to go home. But when Gemma and Perry followed her, she ended up in the library instead. "Why would she lie about going to the library?" Gemma whispered to Perry as the two of them stood shoulder to shoulder against one end of a bookshelf. "It's such a silly thing."

"Maybe she wanted to be alone, but she didn't want to hurt your feelings."

"Why not go home then? Isn't that the perfect place to be alone?"

"Okay, so … maybe she wanted to be alone, but *not* alone at home. Maybe she doesn't feel safe there."

Gemma peeked around the shelf again. Calla sat at a small table between two towering bookshelves. A textbook was open in front of her, but she was staring at the opposite end of the library, her chin resting on her hand. Gemma wished she could see the expression on Calla's face. Wished she could tell if the other girl was still in a strange mood.

"This is wrong," Gemma whispered. "We should just go over there and ask her instead of waiting to see if she uses some kind of dangerous spell. I mean, there's no one else around. She isn't about to rush off for an assignment. We should just *ask*—"

The air seemed to flicker, and then the space on the other side of Calla's table just … disappeared. One moment it was a carpet and empty air and a shelf on either side, and the next moment it was a forest. Calla stood there, along with someone in a white dress and the tattoo artist from Wickedly Inked. Then a blizzard swept across the scene, a million snowflakes blotting out the forest and the people, and then—

It vanished. The library was back. Calla shook her head. She twisted around to look over her shoulder—and Perry yanked Gemma back behind the bookshelf. Gemma grabbed his arm and tugged him away, past another bookshelf and another and another, and then into a row where there was no chance of Calla seeing them. "What. The hell. Was that?" she asked, her voice coming out as a shaky whisper.

"I—I don't know."

"You saw it, right?"

"Yeah."

"Was it … like … a large faerie paths doorway we were looking through?"

"But doorways can't be opened inside the Guild. And even if they somehow could, we saw *her*." Perry pushed a hand through his hair. "But it couldn't be her, because she was sitting right there."

"So it was … some kind of hallucination?"

Perry lifted his shoulders. "I don't know. Maybe."

"Maybe those stories about her are true. Maybe she does make weird things happen to people. "

Perry frowned. "I don't feel any different, though."

"Yeah, me neither. I feel fine. I mean, other than being freaked out." Gemma stared at the floor, her eyebrows pinching together as she tried to figure out what had just happened. She hadn't believed any of the stories about Calla—she still didn't want to—but Calla was definitely hiding something. She was—

Gemma clutched Perry's arm. "Oh my hat. It's so obvious."

Perry looked up. "It is?"

"Yes. She's—" Gemma cut herself off and lowered her voice further. "She's *Griffin Gifted*."

Perry stared at Gemma, then slowly began to nod. "Yeah. She could be."

"She swore to us that she's never made anyone crazy and that she's never used any kind of dark magic, but she didn't deny the stories, and we know she left a number schools. So things definitely happened, and if they weren't a result of suspect magic, then—"

"They were because of a Griffin Ability," Perry finished. "It seems so obvious now. Why hasn't anyone else figured this out?"

Gemma shrugged. "Maybe because half her family is involved with the Guild in some way. No one would suspect them keeping a secret like this from the system they appear to be so loyal to."

"Maybe. Or maybe this has nothing to do with Griffin Abilities."

Gemma tilted her head to the side. "It's possible we're wrong. But I don't think so."

Perry took a deep breath. "What are we gonna do?"

"Well, you know how I feel about the Griffin List."

Perry nodded. "And you know I feel the same way."

"So we do nothing then. And we don't tell Ned. You know how he is about rules and laws."

"Okay," Perry said. "Agreed."

CHAPTER 7

PERRY WAS DRESSED IN THE MOST IDIOTIC OUTFIT EVER, AND he didn't care one bit. In fact, his aim had been to look as silly as possible. The Liberation Day Ball's theme was All Creatures Great and Small, and Perry, who didn't take much in life seriously, wasn't about to start now. Hence the butterfly mask and the wings attached to his back.

He danced through the crowd, either on his own or with anyone who looked like they needed a partner. And all the while, he kept an eye out for Gemma. He wondered what creature she'd dress as and how her outfit would compare to that slinky maroon dress she'd worn to Lucien de la Mer's party. Not that it mattered. Perry had come to realize recently that she looked amazing every day, no matter what she wore. How long had it been since that party? Almost four weeks? And he'd spent every day telling himself that just because Gemma was *attractive* didn't mean he needed to *be attracted to her*. He tried to make himself feel no different than he'd felt before—and then got annoyed when it didn't work.

Man, he was such a girl. He was worse than a girl. Weren't girls the ones who were supposed to agonize over this stuff? Guys were supposed to be all 'Hey, I like you. Let's go out.' That's how he'd acted last year when he asked Misty from the year below him to the Lib Day Ball. She'd said yes, they'd had fun, and they'd dated for a few weeks after that. Then she'd broken up with him because she said he was too friendly with his friends. That the way he acted around 'that girl, Gemma' was basically bordering on ...

"Oh," he said out loud, stopping mid-spin as he remembered Misty's exact words.

Basically bordering on flirting.

Had he really been flirting with Gemma all this time? No. That was silly. It wasn't flirting—which was exactly what he'd told Misty —it was just the way he was. Gemma was a close friend, and he liked to joke around with his friends. Misty hadn't been able to understand that.

He twirled around a few more times, making as many people laugh as possible, before he noticed Calla at the edge of the crowd. He waltzed off the dance floor to greet her. After he bowed and kissed her hand, she said, "You're making fun of this whole dress-up thing, aren't you?"

"Never," he exclaimed. "What makes you think that?"

"I wonder." She reached up and flicked his mask. "And were you dancing by yourself, or did I happen to miss your partner?"

"I was practicing for when the perfect partner comes along."

"I see. Well, your outfit is extraordinary. I think you should win a prize for it."

"Thank you." Perry bowed again. "And may I say that you make a lovely fish, Calla."

Her brows rose as she placed her hands on her hips. "I'm not a fish. I'm a mermaid."

"Oh, sorry, of course. My bad." Perry laughed, but his smile slipped as he focused on someone entering the ballroom. "Is that Gemma?" Her face was covered by a delicate silver mask, and she wore a white, feathery dress. Not stupid feathery, not the kind of feathery he could make fun of, but sleek, elegant feathery that made her look exactly like the swan she was no doubt dressed as.

"Yes, that is Gemma. And that—" Calla added "—is Mr. Perfect. Your competition."

"That's ... whatever ..." Perry spluttered. He focused on the guy on Gemma's arm and practically growled beneath his breath. So this was the guy Gemma had been talking about. And he *did* look perfect, the annoying jerk. His stupid, perfect face was just asking to be punched. Why wasn't he wearing a mask? What was he supposed to be dressed as? Ugh, Perry hated it when people were too cool to make an effort. Now he had to stand next to Mr. Perfect and feel completely foolish. Perry tugged his butterfly mask off and stood a little straighter. It didn't help. He still felt absurd.

Gemma and her date walked over, and Gemma, looking dazed to find herself on the arm of Mr. Perfect Asshat, introduced him as Rick. Perry forced himself to shake the guy's hand. He should probably say something polite, but he couldn't bring himself to do it. If he opened his mouth now, something rude would definitely spill out, and Gemma would never forgive him. Fortunately, Rick asked Gemma to dance then, and the two of them disappeared into the crowd. Perry's shoulders sagged. "Still want to tell me it's not obvious?" Calla said, leaning closer to him.

He continued to stare at his feet, allowing himself an uncharacteristic moment of self-pity. "I suppose it is obvious," he said, finally admitting it out loud. "I only considered it recently, though, the night we came to that party here." He lifted his shoulders before dropping them with a sigh. "I realized afterward that of course I like her. Of course I don't just want to be her friend. But it's too late." He jerked his head over his shoulder and added, "How can I compete with that?"

"You don't have to compete," Calla said. "Just be yourself and tell her how you really feel, and maybe it'll turn out she feels the same way."

He shrugged again, then pushed his shoulders back and straightened. "Well, after rejection like that, all I have left are my dance moves. May I have this dance, Lady Calla?" He held a hand out to her, forcing his misery away.

"Yes, I'd—" She paused, looking past him. "Um, in a minute. Looks like my brother needs me."

"Ah, more rejection," Perry said in anguished tones, pressing a hand dramatically against his chest. "My poor heart can barely stand it."

"Your poor heart will be fine." Calla patted his arm and hugged him briefly before heading away.

Perry looked around, searching for Gemma and then trying not to stare at her once he found her. She and Rick were smiling as they danced—his smile was pompous; hers was nervous—but they didn't appear to be talking at all. How boring. Perry needed a chance with Gemma, just one dance, and he'd show her how much more fun she could have with him than with stale Mr. Perfect. It would probably be tough to pull Gemma off his arm, though, so Perry had to make another plan. He circled the room until he came to the musicians and requested they play the music for a specific dance next. Gemma would have been shocked— "You can't *talk* to them while they're playing!"—and the thought made him smile to himself.

He headed back around the dance floor, looking out for Calla. After spotting her with her brother, he waited nearby until the two of them had finished speaking. "Ready for that dance?" he asked as soon as Ryn walked away. "The next one's about to start and it's my favorite." He put an arm around her shoulders and began guiding her toward the dance floor as the music changed.

"Oh, okay." She looked around. "This is that one where we dance in rows, right? And we keep swapping partners?"

"Yes." Perry looked further down the row to where Gemma was standing opposite Rick. Perfect. Perry may not get an entire dance with Gemma to himself, but he'd get a minute or two, and he planned to make that time count.

Someone near the end of their row counted them in, and everyone started moving. Calla didn't seem entirely familiar with the steps and the hand movements, but Perry was actually a good dancer when he wasn't fooling around, so he made sure she didn't crash into anyone or smack someone in the face.

He spun away from Calla, danced with his second partner, and then finally—*finally*—Gemma was in front of him. "Oh, hey." She smiled at him as their hands moved in the air between them in mirror-image motion.

"Hey. How's your date going? Any sparks flying yet?" He grinned and winked.

"No." She gave him a superior look. "I can control myself, you know."

He grasped her hand and twirled her around—the one and only part of the dance in which he would actually get to touch her. "Well, there can't be much attraction between the two of you if you can control yourself so easily," he said as she turned back to face him. He held onto her hand as he leaned closer to her ear and added, "Shouldn't you guys be setting off fireworks from the mere whisper of each other's names?"

"Shut up!" She pushed him away with a laugh, which didn't wreck the dance since it was time to change partners.

After dancing with a few more people, Perry realized the row was so long that the dance would probably end before he got back to Gemma. He looked around to see who her next partner would be. A short, skinny guy. A third-year trainee? Perry had definitely seen him around. Without pausing to think about it, Perry ducked away from his current partner, grabbed onto the young trainee, said, "Swap with me, will you?" and swung the guy around to take his place.

Just in time for Perry to step in front of Gemma.

"What are you doing?" she asked, her eyes wide. "You're going to ruin the dance."

"So, no sparks," he said, picking up their conversation as if it hadn't ended. "There must be some highly intelligent conversation going on between the two of you then."

"He is smart, but no, we haven't talked much tonight." Beneath the lower edges of her mask, her pink cheeks turned pinker. "I'm so nervous I can't think of anything to say."

"That's your excuse," Perry said, getting some of the hand movements wrong now that he wasn't concentrating properly, "but what's his? If he's as smart as you say, he should be able to come up with a hundred different ways of telling you how pretty you are."

Her gaze moved up to meet his. "You think I look pretty tonight?"

"I think you look pretty all the time, Gem."

Surprise showed in her eyes, but then she was gone again, spinning away from him to join another partner. The dance ended before Perry got another chance with her. The music changed to something slower, something that required two people to stand close together with their arms placed around each other. His heart bounced around erratically at the thought of being so close to Gemma. He wondered if she might possibly say yes to him if he managed to reach her before Rick—

Too late. Mr. Pompous was already taking her hand.

Perry turned away before anyone could see the disappointment on his face. "Hey," said the girl he now found himself in front of. Misty. "Want to dance?" she asked with a shrug. "For old times' sake?"

He smiled. "Okay." No point in wallowing in his dejection. Misty's hands rose to his shoulders. He placed his arms around her. As the dance began, his gaze moved over her shoulder and landed on Gemma. He watched the way she gazed into Rick's eyes and tried not to wish she was staring at him instead.

The dance went on for a painfully long time, and Perry was relieved to get away from Misty when it was over. He moved away from the dance floor and got himself something to eat and drink before he started looking around for Calla. He wandered through the crowd for a while, but he couldn't see her anywhere. He was getting his amber out—and hoping she'd brought hers with—when he noticed the stream of people leaving the ballroom. Curious, he pushed his amber back into his pocket and joined them.

He followed the crowd along a corridor and around a corner to where a large crowd had gathered. He didn't stop to listen to the whispers. He moved quickly, managing to push his way around the edge of the crowd until finally he could see what everyone was staring down at: Saskia. Her skin green and scaly, her eyes unfocused and unblinking.

She was dead.

CHAPTER 8

"Hey, get in here," Perry called as Gemma passed the classroom he was hiding in early Wednesday morning the following week. "Did you hear what happened?"

"Yeah." Gemma ducked into the classroom, slightly breathless. "I was with my mom earlier when they told everyone in the admin department about the quarantine. She's freaking out about not being allowed to leave, and freaking out that she might have made my brothers sick."

"And you?" Perry asked. "Are you freaking out?"

"I ... I don't know." She let her bag slip to the floor. "I think I should be, but it's all a bit of a shock. It's spreading so quickly and nobody knows how to stop it. And what if ... what if my mom or I did take this disease home? What if we've made the rest of our family sick? We could all be dead—the whole Guild could be dead —within a few days."

"So you are freaking out," Perry said. "And you really shouldn't." He moved to put his arm around her, but she stepped away from him, her expression turning to one of annoyance.

"Yes I should. If there was ever a situation that warranted freaking out, it's this one. Why can't you take this seriously?"

"I am taking it seriously. Why do you think I'm hiding in here away from everyone else? I just don't think you need to panic until you know there's definitely something to panic about."

Gemma let out a long breath. "Yeah. Okay." She pushed herself up onto one of the desks. "I wonder if they're still blaming Calla for all of this."

"Idiots," Perry muttered, walking to the door and looking out. "I'm sure they are. They're probably getting ready to upgrade her from suspended to arrested as we speak."

"And the real murderer is somewhere out there laughing at us all from a safe distance."

Perry leaned against the doorway, watching out for any activity and getting ready to put up a shield if someone sick came anywhere near him and Gemma. "And by the time the Council realizes they've been focusing on the wrong person, it'll be far too late."

"I feel sick."

"I know. The whole thing makes me want to throw up. Preferably in the direction of Councilor Merrydale."

"No," she said quietly. "I mean … Perry? My skin is … turning green."

He swung around, fear washing over his body in a wave of goosebumps. Gemma looked at him, her eyes wide, wider than they'd ever been. And her skin … Perry rushed toward her without thinking.

"No!" She raised her hands. Her magic threw him backward, right out the doorway. The door swung shut.

"Gemma!" He scrambled to his feet. He threw himself against the door, beating at it desperately. "Gemma, open the door. Please open the door!"

"No." Her voice was faint. "Don't be silly. You'll end up sick too."

He stopped hitting the door and held his hand over the lock, attempting to open it with magic. No luck. Dammit. He cursed the

169

fact that she'd always known far more spells than he had. "Gemma?"

No answer.

"Gem, please say something. Just so I know you're still …" He couldn't finish the sentence.

"I'm still here," she said.

He slid down until he was sitting on the floor. "You're not going to die," he told her through the door. "Anyone who knows anything about disease spells is working on this thing right now. They could concoct a cure at any moment. There's still time for you."

"You don't know that. My skin is … it's definitely green. And I can see, like … oh, crap, I'm so scared, Perry." Her voice sounded like it was edging toward hysteria. "They look like *scales*, and even if I rub my skin I can't get rid of—"

"Hey, calm down," he said, his voice wavering slightly. "It's fine. You're going to be fine." He pulled out his amber and stylus, and his fingers shook as he wrote a message to Calla.

Gemma's sick. I'm so scared I can't even think properly. I don't know what to do.

He didn't know why he thought Calla might know what to do, but hopefully she could think more clearly than he could right now. Besides, Gemma was her friend, and she needed to know about this. Next, he wrote a similar message to Ned. Ned could usually be counted upon to remain unmoved in emotional situations. He would come up with something. He *had* to come up with something.

"How are you feeling?" Perry asked Gemma, which was such a stupid question, but what else was there to ask in a situation like this?

"Nauseous. Very nauseous."

He tried to distract her then, telling her about whatever meaning-less thing came to mind. What he'd had for breakfast and the new social spell he'd discovered on his amber. Halfway through his description of the movie he'd watched last time he hung out in the human realm, he heard a commotion coming from the direction of the foyer. He pushed himself to his feet. "I'll be right back, okay?" he said to Gemma.

"What?" Her weak voice grew a little stronger. "No, wait, please don't leave me."

"I just need to check what's happening in the foyer. Maybe there's an update on—"

"No! I don't—I don't want to be alone when … when I …"

Perry placed both hands on the door and spoke right into it. "You are not going to die."

He pushed away from the door and ran. When he reached the foyer, he saw several bubble-covered guards struggling with … was that Calla? "… need to take the cure to the healing wing," she was saying. "Please. I'll go wherever you want if you—"

Cure. She'd definitely said cure.

"Our orders are to take you to the Council. Nothing more."

"But people are dying! Please!" Her struggling turned to thrash-ing, but the guards showed no signs of letting go.

"Calla!" Perry shouted as he ran toward her.

"Perry!" She twisted away from one of the guards and dropped to her knees. She fumbled with a pouch, then slid something across the floor as the guard yanked her to her feet again. "Give that to Gemma," she shouted. "Just a drop."

Perry ran for the tiny object sliding toward him—just as a guard collided with him. Perry stumbled to the side and almost fell. He shoved the guy away and kicked him hard, then dove for the object. It was a small glass bottle. He scooped it up before jumping to his feet. His body ached from where he'd hit the marble floor, but he didn't care. He half-ran, half-limped back along the corridor, ready to shoot sparks behind him if he had to fend off a guard. But no one followed him down the corridor.

"Gemma!" he shouted when he reached the door. "Open up. There's a cure. You're gonna be fine."

No answer.

"Gemma?" He banged on the door, but she didn't respond. "Dammit, *dammit*!" he yelled, his voice thick as tears he couldn't control filled his eyes. He wrapped his fingers around the bottle and stepped back. He stood as far across the corridor as he could. Above his open hand, magic began to gather, crackling and sparking and dancing. When he could bear to wait no longer, he threw both the magic and himself at the door.

It slammed open with a deafening bang. Perry crashed into a desk before righting himself and looking wildly around. Gemma lay on the floor to his left. He dropped beside her, already removing the lid from the bottle. Just a drop, Calla had said. With shaking fingers, he held the bottle above Gemma's parted lips, trying not to let too much of the contents fall into her mouth. He put the bottle down, then gently wiped the excess liquid off her lips with his thumb. He pressed his fingers against her neck and felt a faint pulse. The rush of relief was quickly replaced by questions. Was he too late? Was this cure even real? How quickly was it supposed to work?

Belatedly, he realized he should probably take the cure too. He lifted the bottle and let a drop fall onto his tongue before returning his attention to Gemma. He placed a hand on either side of her face and focused on the tiny movements of her eyes behind her closed lids, hoping desperately that some part of her was trying to wake up. "You can't die," he whispered to her. "You can't die, because I love you." His thumbs stroked her pale green skin, and he said the words again and again, as if the mere fact that he loved her might be enough to keep her from dying. It was so stupid—as stupid as anything one might find in those soppy romance novels he sometimes caught Gemma reading—but right now he'd give anything for it to be true. So he took her hand in both of his and squeezed it tight as he told her again that he loved her. And he watched as the scale-like pattern slowly disappeared from her skin and the green tinge began to fade away.

CHAPTER 9

HOLY FREAK. SHE MAY HAVE HAD ONE FOOT ON THE OTHER side of death's doorstep, but Gemma *definitely* heard what Perry said.

I love you. You can't die, because I love you.

By the time she felt alive enough to peel her eyelids apart, other people filled the room. A few guardians, one or two healers. It was tough to tell exactly how many people were there because things seemed to kind of swim across her vision. She wanted to get a better look at Perry's face, but he also kept going in and out of focus. Then he disappeared altogether and she found herself in a bed in the healing wing with her mom quietly weeping beside her. It was another few hours before the healers determined that she and everyone else who had been sick were indeed well. And then at least another hour before she was alone in her bedroom at home and had a moment to try to process what had happened and what Perry had said.

I love you. You can't die, because I love you.

What was she supposed to do with that? He was *Perry*, her annoying best friend, and now suddenly he loved her? And what about Rick? She still had feelings for him—right?

After the Liberation Day Ball, Rick hadn't asked her out. It wasn't that she *expected* him to, but she had *hoped*, of course. She had hoped he would finally notice her as more than just another girl who followed him around. She had hoped he might kiss her goodnight, at least. She'd imagined it so many times, her first kiss …

But the tragedy with Saskia had happened, and Rick and Gemma's parting had been a hasty one. And that was after he'd turned out to be kinda boring at the ball itself. Seriously, didn't he have anything to *say*? Could it be that the only thing they ever spoke about was their training? And why hadn't he made an effort to dress to the theme? She hated it when people didn't make an effort for things like that. But he was still Rick and she still liked him, didn't she?

She had worried for days after the ball that Perry might be right. That perhaps there was zero attraction between her and Rick. And then Perry had to go and say he *loved* her and complicate things even further! And while she was *dying*! She'd been in dangerous situations before, of course, but nothing had ever come close to the utter terror she felt this morning knowing for certain that this was the end.

But then it wasn't.

And Perry loved her.

And her family was alive and healthy.

And it was all just exhausting.

She lay awake for a long time that night, trying to figure out how she felt and what she should say to Perry, but eventually her fatigue consumed her. Morning brought her no closer to an answer, and when her mom shouted up the stairs before they left for the Guild that Perry was there to see her, she almost shouted back that she didn't feel well enough for visitors. But that wasn't fair. If Perry had made the effort to get out of bed this early, he must still be worried about her. Pretending she didn't feel well would only increase his concern—and her mom's. Besides, he had *saved her life*. No matter how muddled up she felt about his declaration of love, she needed to tell him how unendingly grateful she was.

She checked her appearance in the mirror—why? She didn't usually care what she looked like in front of Perry—and descended the stairs. He was leaning against a couch, smiling as he looked toward the kitchen where her brothers were playing a game with their breakfast, and her mom was trying to calm them down. "Wow, you're up early," she joked as she reached the bottom step.

He looked at her. He stood up. Then he was across the room and hugging her, tighter than he'd ever hugged her before. But not tight in a constricting way. Tight in a way that made her feel safe. It was exactly the kind of hug she needed yesterday when she was alone in that classroom, waiting to ... to die.

"Sorry," he said, his smile appearing again as he stepped back. "It's just ... the last time I saw you, I wasn't sure yet if you were okay."

"I am," she said, returning his smile but not quite meeting his gaze. "I'm fine. And thank you," she added hurriedly. "Thank you *so much*. For being there, on the other side of the door. For talking to me the whole time. And then for getting the cure. And for forcing the door open. I used the strongest locking spell I knew, but I guess I underestimated your strength."

"I think you underestimated my desperation," he said with a laugh.

"Yeah, well, thank you." Her hands twisted together as she focused her gaze somewhere in the region of his chin. She couldn't look any higher. She was too damn scared of what she might see in his eyes.

* * *

Perry waited for her to mention that part. He waited for her to say, 'That love stuff was a joke, right?' or 'Sooooo, I need some time to think about what you said,' or 'This is awkward, but I just don't feel the same way.' But she didn't so much as hint at the fact that he'd admitted he loved her. And finally he realized, with both relief and disappointment, that she hadn't heard him. Of course she hadn't. She'd been close to death at that point, so what did he expect? That she was paying close attention to every word he said? Of course not.

Unless ... no. She wouldn't pretend she hadn't heard him, would she? But she was acting a little strange. She wouldn't look him in the eye, so ... crap. She must have heard him. He should say something now. Get it all out in the open. Except ... if she *had* heard him and decided to say nothing about it, that could mean only one thing: she didn't feel the same way.

He tugged at his hair as she hurried back upstairs to fetch her bag. "You idiot," he muttered to himself. He shouldn't have said anything. He should have just given her the cure without the whole 'I love you' crap. But he hadn't been able to help himself. The words had just tumbled out of him. And now, because he couldn't keep his feelings to himself, he had to figure out how to be friends with someone he was without a doubt in love with.

CHAPTER 10

It was Sunday. Gemma wasn't supposed to be at the Guild. Neither was her mom—she didn't often work on Sundays—but everyone wanted to know what the heck was happening after yesterday's battle on Velazar Island. Gemma had only discovered something was going on last night after her mom received a call from one of her admin friends who had a Saturday shift. Gemma and her mom had then sat up half the night contacting everyone they knew in their attempt to find out more. Perry hadn't replied to Gemma's message. Neither had Ned. Her terrified mind kept telling her they must have gone off to Velazar Island to join the fight without her, but she was probably overreacting. They would have told her about something that major. Besides, trainees weren't supposed to get involved in things like this, and Ned liked to follow the rules.

So now Gemma's mother had gone off to the Guild without her, saying things would be chaotic and Gemma would only get in the way. Somehow her mother was exempt from this getting-in-the-way theory. Gemma argued until her mom finally agreed to mirror-call her every time she discovered something new.

Gemma couldn't sit still, so she paced the living room with a mirror under her arm while her brothers sat on the floor playing cards. She'd tried getting hold of Perry and Ned again this morning, but neither of them answered her calls or messages. She wondered if she was allowed to start freaking out yet. She wanted to rush over to Perry's house and find out if he was just being super lazy and sleeping late, but her dad was working today and Jazz wasn't around, so Gemma couldn't leave her brothers at home alone.

She did another circuit around the living room. She'd been hearing Perry's words over and over for hours now—*you can't die, because I love you*—until eventually they felt like her words as well, and not just his. That was silly, though. It probably wasn't true. Her emotions were just overreacting to the situation. Which might, she realized now, have been what happened to Perry when she got sick. The near-death situation had made him *think* that he loved her.

At least she'd figured out her feelings where Rick was concerned. She'd had a month to think about it now and had discovered that her long-time crush on him had kind of ... fizzled away. She'd always thought of him as the perfect guy, but it turned out perfect was kinda boring. He was polite, intelligent, and ridiculously good-looking. He smiled a lot but ... he didn't really make her laugh. He'd started dating another Seer trainee in his class about a week ago, and Gemma had tried to make herself feel upset about it. But then she was paired against Perry in the Fish Bowl, and that was all she could think about, both before and after the session.

She thought about it again now. She thought about *him* and the possibility that she'd never see him in the training center again, never hug or speak to or laugh with him. She considered him simply being *gone*—and she felt utterly devastated. She imagined the same thing happening to Ned, but as awful as that would be—and of course it would be horribly tragic if Ned died—it didn't feel awful in the same way.

You can't die, because I love you.

I think you look pretty all the time, Gem.

Gem. He hardly ever, *ever* called her that, and she realized now that she loved it. That it made her feel precious, like a jewel, like something rare and special. And what if she never heard him say her name like that again?

She stopped pacing. "Get up," she told her brothers. "Put your shoes on. We're going out." She would go to Perry's house right now and find out for certain if something had happened to him. And when it turned out that he'd simply overslept, she was going to give him a serious piece of her mind for making her worry so much. And then, if she was brave enough, she might admit she'd heard him telling her he loved her and that they should probably talk about it.

She'd just gotten her brothers ready to leave when she heard a knock from outside. She almost tripped over her own feet in her haste to get to the wall. She fumbled with her stylus and opened a doorway.

"Hey," Ned said.

"Ned!" Relief washed over her, followed closely by annoyance. "Didn't you see all the messages I sent you?"

"Yeah, I saw them when I woke up. There were a lot, so I thought I'd just come over here and show you I'm fine."

Gemma groaned and stepped back to let him in. She would have hugged him, but he wasn't really the hugging type.

"Has Perry talked to you today?" Ned asked.

Gemma's insides tightened again. "No. I haven't heard from him. I figured you'd know where he was. Oh hell, do you think something happened to him?"

"No, I'm sure he's fine. It's just that we had a disagreement last night, so I was wondering if he's come to his senses yet."

"Oh." A weak laugh escaped her. "I thought maybe … the fight last night …"

"Yeah, we were there," Ned said, nodding. "Pretty insane."

Her mouth dropped open. "You were there? But ... you didn't ..." She shook her head. *"You were there?"*

"Yes." He frowned, as if there was something wrong with *her*, not him. "We were at the Guild when all the guardians left for Velazar, so Perry said we should go with them because they'd need as much help as possible. And then at the end—" Ned's brow creased further as he sat on the arm of a couch "—when all the Griffin Gifted were revealed, Perry started *helping* them get away instead of capturing them. And he was riding a *gargoyle*. Can you believe it? Those creatures are bound to the Unseelie Court, and he decided to just get on one like it was no big deal. I don't know if anyone from the Guild saw him helping the Gifted, but if they did, he's going to be in serious trouble. I mean, where exactly do his loyalties lie?"

Horrifying images flashes through Gemma's mind. "So—so he's okay?"

"Yeah, the idiot's fine. I mean, he got banged up during the fight, but we all did. I'm sure he's back to normal now."

"That's ... that's good." Her words came out as a hoarse whisper as tears sprang up in her eyes.

"Are you ..." Ned's eyes widened. He stood quickly "Um ... I ... I think I'm gonna go now."

"No," she blurted out. "Can you—can you stay with my brothers? Watch them until I get back?"

"Uh, okay."

"Thanks." She rushed to the wall again, but this time she opened a doorway to the paths instead of outside. She arrived at Perry's house seconds later. His mom opened a doorway for her and told her Perry wasn't home. "He's been at the Guild all morning. Oh, and his amber broke last night. He's using an old one. He left before giving me the ID, so you'll have to get it from him."

"Okay, thanks." A few minutes later, Gemma was running around the Guild searching for Perry. Her mother was right about it being chaotic here. She kept having to step around people. Eventually, after searching almost every accessible level of the Guild, someone from her class said Perry had mentioned going to the old Guild ruins.

"He had damn well better be there," she muttered to herself as she left through the Guild's entrance room. Light appeared at the other end of the faerie paths, and she stepped out onto the ruins.

And there he was.

Relief hit her the moment she saw him. But he was so at ease, so completely unaware of the nightmare he'd put her through, that anger flared up and burned through her relief. "What the hell, Perry?" she yelled.

He looked at her, and his smile slipped a little. He glanced away for a moment, then back at her. "Um …"

"Ned just visited." Gemma stomped across the ruins toward Perry. "He told me about last night. You two were *there*! And you didn't tell me it was happening or that you were going!"

"Well … it was dangerous."

"I KNOW!" she shouted, tears pricking behind her eyes again. "That's my point. You could have died!"

"You know we're training to be guardians, right?" he said carefully. "The possibility of death is always—"

Without another thought, Gemma closed the distance between them. She stood on tiptoe, threw her arms around him, and pressed her lips to his. He remained frozen for several seconds, and she wondered if she'd made a mistake—if she'd waited too long, if he'd never actually meant 'I love you'—but then his hands slid around her and pulled her closer. He sighed against her lips, and her body went soft and pliant, fitting perfectly against his. Her lips tingled, and her heart pumped equal parts exhilaration and terror, because *she'd never done this before*! She was hyperaware of everything, his hands trailing down her back, her fingers twining in his hair, their mouths moving against each other. It was possible she was terrible at this and just didn't know it, but she wouldn't stop as long as it felt this good.

She didn't know how much time passed before they slowed, but she needed to catch her breath, and it sounded like Perry did too. She pulled back a little and looked down, letting her forehead rest against his. He didn't say anything and neither did she, and she wondered if things were going to be eternally awkward now. After all, she had just made out with one of her best friends. That kinda thing generally resulted in awkwardness, right?

She bit her lip, her cheeks growing hotter than they already were. Perry moved back a bit. She could sense him watching her, so she dared—finally dared—to look up and meet his eyes. "You so totally love me," he said with a grin. "I knew it."

And just like that, things weren't awkward. "Shut up," she said, trying not to smile. "You knew nothing."

He kissed her again, and it was so weird and so right. "Admit it," he said, his brow resting against hers once more.

"Fine. Of course I love you, you idiot."

He laughed. "That's not quite the way I was hoping to hear it, but I'll take it."

She closed her eyes and let herself smile. "I love you," she whispered.

He kissed her again.

TREASURE HUNT

This story takes place roughly six months after *Rebel Faerie*, the final book in the Creepy Hollow series, and is essentially an 'extended epilogue' featuring all the main characters.

Read it any time after *Rebel Faerie*,
Creepy Hollow Book Nine.

CHAPTER 1

High above the Topaz Sea amid a cluster of small floating islands that vaguely resembled misshapen, weatherworn dragons, Emerson Larkenwood clung to a vine. Her gaze was pointed directly upward at the crumbling, craggy side of the highest island. She frowned, bit her lip, and wiggled a little, forcing the vine to sway slightly. It remained securely attached to the side of the island, which was great—she didn't particularly feel like plummeting toward the ocean far below—but it didn't solve her problem.

The giant spider. Or at least, the creature that *looked* something like a giant spider. It was black and hairy with bright silver spots covering its bulbous body, and had numerous hairy legs. It also appeared to possess the ability to wrap itself snuggly around a skinny vine while sleeping. Well, Em assumed it was sleeping. She had tugged the vine multiple times, and the spider had stubbornly refused to move.

"I'm pretty sure it's poisonous," said a voice from below Em.

"What? How sure?"

"Mm … like eighty-eight percent sure."

Em looked down, forcing her gaze to stay on the ruffled pink and blond head just beneath her feet and not on the sparkling blue sea very, very, *very* far below. "That's alarmingly close to a hundred."

"Yeah …" Tilly said. "So we have two options."

A cool breeze curled past, blowing a few loose strands of Em's hair across her face. Angling her head to the side, she attempted to nudge the hair away from her eyes using only her shoulder. No way was she about to remove a hand from this vine. "I'm hoping," she said to Tilly, "that at least one of these options includes not dying."

Tilly's lips stretched into a grin. "Where's the fun in that?"

Em couldn't help smiling in response. "There's a part of me that agrees with you, but there's also the part that remembers you promised no life-threatening situations."

"Hmm. True." Tilly's grin slipped a little. "We probably shouldn't tell your mother about this."

Guilt nudged at the back of Em's mind. Up until now, it had been fairly easy to follow Vi's 'no life-threatening situations' instruction. And even at the start of today's little adventure, it hadn't occurred to Em that she and Tilly might be putting their lives at risk.

They'd used the faerie paths to get to the lowest island, and then again to get to an island higher up. Pretty easy, no obstacles. But then they'd reached a point where the paths no longer seemed to be accessible, and they'd started climbing up using the vines hanging below the islands. It was only when they were dangling in midair with a possibly poisonous spider above them that Em realized they were in danger. "We *definitely* shouldn't tell Vi about this," she agreed. "Or Ryn."

"*Technically*, there's nothing to tell," Tilly pointed out, "since nothing has threatened our lives yet."

"And if something *does* threaten our lives, they probably shouldn't blame you for it, since I'm the one who urged you to go on this little side quest." When Em and Tilly had been lying in hammocks this morning on a beach that was the very definition of paradise and Tilly's amber had started singing her name, Em had asked if everything was okay.

"It's from Jayshu," Tilly had said, referring to one of her colleagues. "'Got your next project lined up for you,'" she read out. "'I'm busy with the new exhibit, but you can probably handle it on your own. An ancient magical book supposedly containing the location of an equally ancient treasure. Scrolls I just translated suggest the book is sitting on top of a hill on the highest island in a constellation of levitating islands. Director gave us the go-ahead. Coordinates to follow.'" Tilly had turned her head to the side and looked at Em. "Well now. Doesn't that sound interesting."

Tilly worked for the Museum of Mysterious Magical Artifacts, so everything she did sounded interesting to Em. Her official job title was something boring Em couldn't remember, but she was, in essence, a professional adventurer.

"Sounds very interesting indeed," Em said. "Did he send you the coordinates?"

Tilly looked at her amber again. "Yep."

"So ... today is our last vacation day ... and tomorrow you take me back home ..."

"Yes, and the following day is my first day back at work."

"So you'll head off on this adventure to find an ancient book and an ancient treasure."

"Correct. Well, there'll probably be some boring paperwork I have to catch up on, but if I can put that off for a few days, then yes. I'll head off on this little expedition immediately."

"Or ..." Em said slowly.

Tilly met her gaze and arched a brow. One side of her mouth lifted in a mischievous smile. "Are you thinking what I'm thinking, Miss Emerson-Victoria?"

Em would have rolled her eyes at the name Tilly had given her if she hadn't heard it a hundred times already over the past month. "If you're thinking that you're bored out of your mind sitting on this beach and would prefer to go on a little treasure hunt, then yes."

A wide grin split Tilly's face. "I knew I liked you the moment I met you."

Em moved to climb out of her hammock, then paused. "It's unlikely to be life-threatening, right?"

"Life-threatening? Pffft. Never. What could be life-threatening about a book?"

Em thought for a moment, then decided not to jinx things by answering that.

"Still," Tilly said as she swung her legs over the side of her hammock, "I should probably be a responsible adult and tell you to lie back down and ignore the exciting idea of a quest for ancient treasure."

Em stared at her, raised an eyebrow, and snorted. "Really? You're going to tell me that?"

Tilly laughed. "I don't think I could force the words past my lips if I tried."

"Awesome." Em jumped to her feet. "Because it would be terribly tragic to spend our last vacation day doing nothing but lying in a hammock."

Now, dangling a bajillion feet above the sea with no way of quickly escaping into the faerie paths and confronted by the very real threat of being bitten by a magical spider, lying in a hammock was starting to look more than a little appealing. Em's arm and thigh muscles, which were starting to shake with the effort of keeping her attached to the vine, agreed. Thank goodness for the minuscule gloves Tilly had whipped out of one of the hollow pendants on her charm bracelet and enlarged to the correct size for Em. Enchanted with some kind of magical grip, they were probably the only reason Em hadn't slipped yet.

"Nothing is going to threaten our lives," Tilly assured her. "Like I said, we have two options. Well, three if you include the possibility of using your Griffin Ability to tell the spider to move. But who knows how long we'd have to wait for—"

"And there's the fact that I'm not supposed to use it anymore," Em added.

"Right, yes. Long-term side-effects and all that. Not ideal while hanging high above the ocean."

"Definitely not ideal," Em agreed. She'd experienced some extreme dizziness after using her Griffin Ability so much during the whole magical-invasion-of-the-human-world thing. But she'd been told it was due to overuse of the elixir that artificially stimulated her Griffin Ability, and once it was gone, she'd assumed she was fine.

But then the dizziness struck again a few days later, and then again a week after that. When it happened yet *again*—this time while riding a gargoyle and almost falling off—Vi and Ryn strongly suggested she not use her Griffin Ability at all for a while. It had been several months now, and the alarming dizziness hadn't returned.

"So here are the two options," Tilly continued. "One, we climb past the spider and hope it doesn't bite us. Or two, we use a little magic to get this vine swinging, grab onto that vine all the way over there, and climb up that way instead."

"So basically," Em said, "we have one option. Because there's no way I'm using a giant hairy venomous spider as climbing apparatus. That's not the kind of adrenaline rush I'm after."

"We could always turn back," Tilly pointed out. "That's an option too."

"That seems …" *Like the safest option. The option my parents, who I know were massive risk-takers when they were my age, would tell me to choose.* "Like giving up?" Em finished out loud.

"It does seem a little like giving up when we're so close," Tilly admitted, "but I don't want to end up on Vi and Ryn's bad side if something goes wrong. So perhaps we should—Oh. Uh, never mind."

"What?" Em peered down but couldn't see past Tilly to whatever Tilly was looking at.

"There's another one. Climbing up. Man, that's quite impressive. You'd think that with so many legs and such a large body, it wouldn't be so easy for it to—Oh, I can see this one's mouth. Are those ... fangs? Oh, it's moving faster. Much faster."

Em muttered a curse beneath her breath. *Dash wouldn't approve of that*, she thought the moment the word escaped her lips—and then immediately reminded her brain not to think about Dash. Her stomach churned, guilt and regret jostling for space alongside her fear.

Don't. Think. About. Him.

Her fingers ached as she tightened her grip on the vine. "Okay, so we're definitely not climbing back down."

"Nope," Tilly agreed. "Let's start swinging. I'll try to get us moving quickly, just in case the first spider slips down and falls on your head."

"What?"

"Kidding. Kind of. There was this one time when an ice-spitting lizard landed on my shoulder, but it was a lot smaller than—"

"You're not helping, and we really need to get moving—"

"Okay, here we gooooo!" Tilly removed one gloved hand from the vine, tugged the glove off with her teeth, and threw her arm outward. Magic escaped her hand in a rush of sparks, shoving her backward along with the vine and Em—and the spider above Em that was hopefully hanging on just as tightly.

They reached the highest point of their trajectory, motionless for a single moment, and then Em's stomach dropped as they began swinging back in the other direction. She resisted the urge to clamp her eyelids shut. She kinda needed to see what was happening if she was hoping to grab hold of another vine.

"Aaaaand ... not quite close enough," Tilly called out as they slowed, paused, and began swinging back again, away from the vine they were aiming for. "Jeepers, that spider down there is getting close," she added.

"Just don't let it—" Em's words were lost as Tilly let out a bloodcurdling screech. Em gripped the vine so tightly she thought her fingers might break. Her heart hammered painfully in her chest. "What the holy heck was that?" she demanded when Tilly had finished screaming.

"Just letting him know who's boss," Tilly replied calmly. "Okay, I'm giving us an extra burst of magic." Sparks exploded in the air again, pushing them higher this time before they reached that weightless moment. Em exhaled shakily as they began their descent, faster now than the previous time. "I think we're going too fast. What if we swing right past—"

"When I say 'now,' let go of this vine and grab the other one."

"Wait, I'm not—"

"Now!"

CHAPTER 2

THE ENTIRE PLAN HINGED ON A BAGEL. SIMPLE ENOUGH, BUT Calla should have known the plan was heading south when she arrived at Chase's favorite bagel spot in the human realm and found they'd just sold the last one. Honestly, what kind of bagel place *sold out* of bagels? Shouldn't they have an endless supply?

She curbed her disappointment and reminded herself that the exact *type* of bagel wasn't the important part. All that mattered was that there *was* one. So she asked where else she could find bagels and ended up a few blocks down at a corner cafe that didn't look nearly as popular. She decided not to mention exactly where the bagel had come from and wait to see if Chase noticed. He probably wouldn't. Not after the news she planned to share with him.

The second thing to go wrong was a sharp knock on her front door late in the afternoon just as she'd finished putting together the table setting. She had the rest of the day off, Chase was out meeting a client, and no one was supposed to be interrupting her. She stared across the room that served as an entrance area, sitting room, *and* dining room, and contemplated ignoring whoever was standing on the other side of the door.

Another knock.

With a great deal of effort, Calla resisted the urge to head for the door and pull it open. She just needed to remain silent another few seconds, and whoever was trying to get her attention would—

A third knock.

—would *not* give up, apparently. With a sigh, Calla crossed the room to the door and tugged it open. A twilight sky was visible between the leaves and branches of the gargantuan tree her home was built into, and a few glow-bugs had already popped out. It was later than she'd realized.

"Ana?" she said at the sight of the petite, breathless elf standing in her doorway. "Is everything okay?"

"Yeah, I tried to get you on your amber, but—" deep breath "—you weren't responding. I tried to mirror call a bunch of times too." Another deep breath, this one accompanied by a particularly grumpy look. As if it were Calla's fault she'd had to climb the lengthy curving stairway carved around the trunk of this tree. "The Carroways are demanding to meet with you this evening."

Calla frowned. "Isn't their meeting scheduled for tomorrow evening? And I thought Chase was the one meeting with them."

"Well, yes, but they said they have a problem and it's urgent." Ana crossed her tattooed arms over her chest and sighed. "Stolen documents containing sensitive information."

"Again?"

"I know, right? They really should be paying for better security with all that money they seem to have. Anyway, they're worried about whose hands this info will fall into. And they have reasons— as always—for not wanting to go to the Guild for help. Griffin List stuff. Since Chase isn't available, I figured you could handle it."

"I'm not available either. I have the rest of the day off."

"Oh." Ana looked confused. Understandable, since Calla didn't often take time off, and when she did, she would happily fill in for someone else if there was an issue that urgently needed to be dealt with. But she wasn't giving in this time.

"Isn't there someone else available to meet with them?"

"I … guess?" Ana played absently with one of her many ear piercings. "I mean … I could go?"

"Oh." Calla's desire for personal time dropped from the top of her priority list in the face of her rising panic. No way could she let dry, sarcastic Ana meet with one of their most sensitive, high-maintenance clients.

"Kidding," Ana said with a roll of her eyes, letting her hand drop to her side. "I don't do people. I'll send Darius."

"Um—"

"Kidding again." Ana shuddered. "That would be even worse."

Though she wasn't about to say it out loud, Calla agreed with her. "Isn't there anyone else around? If not, the Carroways will just have to wait until tomorrow. I can probably meet with them in the morning."

"Nah, don't worry, I'm sure I can find someone who's available now."

Calla crossed her own tattooed arms over her chest. They weren't nearly as inked as Ana's, but she loved the swirling, leafy design that wound its way up her left arm and ended on the side of her neck, as well as the elegant script on the inside of her right arm. "You didn't think to look for someone before you climbed alllll the way up here to find me?"

Ana stuck her pierced tongue out, then said, "Maybe I missed you."

It was Calla's turn to roll her eyes. "Uh huh. Sure." At some point in the months after Calla had become entangled in Chase's world, Ana and Calla had stopped tiptoeing around one another and become genuine friends. They'd grown close over the years, and Calla now thought of her as something like a sister. An annoying, grumpy one, but still someone she loved as much as her own family.

"Well, anyway …" Ana's gaze shifted past her, and she raised an eyebrow. "Are you planning a date night or something?"

Calla tried to stand a little taller in an attempt to block Ana's view of the space behind her, though it was clear she'd already spotted the table. "I am, so that's why I can't—"

"A bagel? *That's* what you're using for a centerpiece?"

Calla sighed and slowly turned to face the table on the other side of the room. It was usually covered in sketchbooks, colored pencils, enchanted paintbrushes, and loose pages decorated with doodles and half-finished drawings. But today she'd cleaned everything up, dug out a table runner—a gift from Raven made of fabric that changed color to best suit the surrounding items—and added a few candles and trailing jasmine. The runner had decided to change itself from black—a color which presumably matched the inside of the box it had found itself stored in for years—to silver that sparkled faintly in the candlelight. It all looked quite lovely.

Well, aside from the random single bagel sitting on an antique silver cake stand in the center of the table. Which was none of Ana's business, despite the are-you-kidding-me look she'd been directing at Calla before Calla turned away.

"You guys are *way* too obsessed with those things," Ana said. "Seriously, if you're not eating them, you're talking about how much you want them, or arguing about whether you're ready for them, or having emotional crises about the responsibility of … Oh." She stopped. She paused. Calla held her breath, hoping Ana hadn't just figured out— "'Bagel' is a code word, isn't it."

"Okay!" Calla said in an overly bright tone, spinning back around and steering Ana toward the door. "Time for you to go."

"What does the bagel mean, Calla?" Ana demanded, even as Calla pushed her over the threshold. "I mean, I'm pretty sure I know what the word *represents*, but what's the significance of an actual bagel sitting in the middle of your dinner table? Does it mean that you're—"

Calla banged the door shut.

"I know you can still hear me!" Ana called from the other side of the door. "Congratulations, by the way. In general, I don't really like 'bagels,' but I'm sure I can make an exception for any 'bagel' that belongs to you and Chase!"

"Go away!" Calla called back, but there was a smile on her lips and laughter in her voice. She leaned forward and pressed her forehead against the door, closing her eyes and letting out a sigh. Well *that* certainly hadn't been part of the plan. No one else was supposed to know before she told Chase. At least it was Ana, though, who was kind of like a little sister to Chase too. He'd known her since she was a teenager on the run from the Guild. And she wasn't the gossipy type. She would keep the news to herself.

Calla stepped away from the door, a frown in place as her brain stuck on Ana's use of the word *arguing*. That part wasn't quite right. She and Chase weren't *arguing* about 'bagels.' It wasn't as though one of them wanted 'bagels' and the other didn't. It was more the fact that Calla had never quite been able to forgive herself for the part she'd played in the death of Vi and Ryn's first 'bagel,' and Chase was under the impression that because of who he was and what he'd done, he was the very last person on earth who should be allowed to raise his own 'bagel.'

So both of them had spent years dealing with their own fears and doubts while constantly trying to convince the other that they had no real reason for *their* fears and doubts. And they had never managed to get to a point where they felt that 'bagels' were the right thing for them. Even after Vi and Ryn had Jack.

And then Em had arrived and Calla had figured out who she was. And finally, *finally* she had found herself released of that last shard of guilt that had burrowed its way deep into her heart that terrible night all those years ago when everyone thought tiny Victoria Rose Larkenwood had died.

Something had changed for Chase too. There was something

about Vi and Ryn getting their presumed-to-be-deceased daughter back—a happy ending no one ever even knew they could wish for —that seemed to give him renewed hope about the world. Good could still come out of bad. Joy and light could still exist after darkness and suffering. He had known this before. He had helped countless people since he'd decided to drag himself out of the depths of his misery and try to make a difference in the world. And yet none of it had had as much of an impact on him as *this*: Em finding her way home to the family she didn't even know she had.

So Chase and Calla had spoken about 'bagels' yet again—in code, because everyone around them was so darn nosy, and sometimes these conversations didn't happen in the privacy of their own home—and it seemed they'd both finally reached some kind of peace about the idea.

Calla had quite the feast planned for dinner tonight, and she needed to get started immediately if she was hoping to get it all done before Chase got home. And that meant … She turned on the spot, looking for her little hand mirror. Where had she left it? She needed to call Gaius so he could talk her through the steps of making those fancy chocolate-caramel domes he was so good at. She'd only attempted them once before, and they'd turned out a mess.

She walked to the bedroom, making a mental note on the way to search the kitchen cupboards for the silver cloche she'd borrowed from her mother years ago and cover the bagel with it until it was reveal time. She found her bag on the bed and dug through it until her fingers curved around the mirror. Small and round, it fit easily into her palm.

She was just about to call Gaius when the mirror began to hum a friendly tune and Ryn's face showed on the surface. With a sigh, Calla tapped the glass. "Hey, what's up?"

"Hi." Ryn's head was too close to the mirror for her to figure out where he might be. "Are you … okay?"

Calla frowned. "Yes, I'm fine. Why wouldn't I be?"

"You've just been … different the past few days."

She groaned. "For the millionth time, you know I hate it when you do that."

"For the millionth time," he replied, "you know I can't help it."

"Well you should do what you usually do and pretend you didn't feel anything."

Ryn rubbed the side of his neck. "Yeah, I probably should do that. I'm sorry. It just seemed like you were excited about something."

"Stop prying!"

"I'm not prying!"

Calla narrowed her eyes at him. "Where are you?"

"The top of our tree. Waiting for Vi."

Calla looked across the bedroom and out of the window. Between the branches, she could just make out the neighboring mammoth of a tree where Ryn and Vi and several other families lived. "So you're bored. You only ever call me when you have nothing else to do."

"Because I see you in person pretty much every day."

"Okay I'm going now," Calla said, dropping the mirror onto the bed.

"Wait!" Ryn called out, and Calla dropped onto the side of the bed with another groan. She picked up the mirror. "Do you guys want to have dinner with us tonight?" he asked. "We might have some news to share."

"What?" No doubt because of her entirely 'bagel'-focused mind, Calla immediately assumed that Ryn was referring to the same type of news she was planning to share with Chase tonight. No, no, no, *no*. That was not the way tonight was supposed to go.

"Work news. Guild news."

"Oh." Calla almost rolled her eyes. Of course it wasn't *'bagel'* news. "What does that mean?"

"Just … I'm not sure yet. Anyway, do you and Chase want to come over for dinner?"

"We can't."

"Oh, I thought you both had the evening off."

"We do. But we're busy. Bye, big brother!" She blew a kiss at him, then waved her hand over the mirror's surface to end the call. She breathed out a long sigh as she headed back to the living room. Wrong type of bagel, Ana figuring out her secret, Ryn attempting to butt his way into her plans for tonight. What other problems would she have to deal with before she eventually got to share her exciting news?

She shouldn't have let the thought take form, because that was precisely when the fourth thing went wrong: The front door crashed open and Chase stumbled inside covered in blood.

CHAPTER 3

"See?" Tilly said to Em. "That was easy. And I'm pretty sure I scared the spider off with my scream."

Em swung her legs over the rock she'd just pulled herself up and took several long strides away from the edge of the floating island. She'd spent years doing somersaults and flips, leaping over rooftops and walls, and cartwheeling her way across roads and parking lots, but the town she'd grown up in had precisely zero vines from which to swing. Letting go of one and grabbing hold of another was not what she would call *easy*. "I think I need a little more practice," she said to Tilly.

"Hang around me long enough and you'll get plenty of practice," Tilly said with a dismissive wave. She looked around. "Okay, let's find this book. Shouldn't take us long."

Em looked past her. The island they stood on was … a hill. That was it. Well, she couldn't be certain what was on the other side of the hill, but she'd seen the island from beneath, so she knew it wasn't large enough to hold much more. "I guess we're heading up there," she said, pointing to the top of the hill.

"Yep. I say we pick up the book and head straight back to that beach with the hammocks and those drinks with the little enchanted umbrellas. I'll save the actual treasure hunting for after I've returned you safely to your family."

Em bit back the urge to grumble. The treasure was the part she was most interested in, but if something happened to her, Vi and Ryn might never forgive Tilly, and Em didn't want to be the reason they stopped speaking to one of their oldest friends. "Probably a good idea," she said as they began climbing. The terrain was mostly rocky and bare, with the occasional shrub protruding from among the loose stones. She couldn't imagine there being many living creatures up here. *Although* ... She frowned at the loose pebbles. This was the fae world. There might be all kinds of strange beings inhabiting this floating island.

"Sooooo," Tilly said, "now that we're not facing death and are free to *talk* ..."

This time, Em didn't bother holding back her groan. This was one of the reasons she'd been so excited to get out of that hammock this morning. It wasn't just that staring at the inside of a pair of sunglasses while sipping a magically never-ending drink out of half a coconut was starting to grow boring. It was that Tilly had just asked her if she wanted to talk about Dash, and Em had been trying to figure out the politest way to say no.

"Come on," Tilly coaxed. "I feel like I've been *super* patient. I haven't pressed you for details the entire time we've been traveling together. I figured you'd open up on your own at some point. But we're heading back tomorrow, and you still haven't breathed a word."

"Well, you know ... perhaps I don't *want* to breathe a word about it." Em tucked the loose strands of her hair behind both ears, trying—and failing—not to mentally relive the way she'd epically messed things up.

After everything that had happened since the moment she first arrived in the fae world, she'd been so excited to begin the life she was always meant to live. She'd thrown herself into her lessons, continued weapons training, helped out around the oasis in whatever way she could, asked endless questions about her family history, and attended every counseling session Vi and Ryn had gently forced on her. She'd thought everything was perfect.

And then ...

Dash.

When their relationship had gone up in a literal blazing inferno along with the pavilion inside the oasis, Vi and Ryn had decided it might be a good time for Em to do some of that exploring she kept talking about. They'd dragged Tilly away from whatever jungle or mountain or cave she was currently exploring and politely begged her to let Em tag along for a while.

"Perfect timing," Tilly had told them. "My boss keeps reminding me that I've accumulated too many vacation days and need to use them or lose them."

"Absolutely *no* life-threatening situations," Vi had insisted. "Just ... do a little sightseeing. Show Em what else is out there."

"Awesome. I can take a month off and we'll visit all my favorite non-hostile spots around the world."

Ryn had frowned at the phrase 'non-hostile,' and Violet had seemed to choke on something when Tilly used the word 'month.' But she'd taken a deep breath and told Tilly that was a great plan, then tried to hide her tears when, a week later, it came time to say goodbye for a month.

"You know, I can come back here every night," Em had pointed out. "It's quick through the faerie paths. We don't have to say goodbye like we won't see each other for weeks."

"No, no, I think you need a real break," Vi said, and Ryn—after doing one of those silent communication glances he and Vi seemed to be so good at—nodded in agreement. "Stop the studying, stop the training. Just be a tourist."

"Besides," Ryn added. "The faerie paths aren't always accessible in some of those particularly remote areas."

"But, you know, you should try to avoid those areas," Vi said, giving Tilly a pointed look. "Because if you happen to need help, we won't be able to get to you."

"We won't need help," Tilly assured her. "We'll be going on bubble rides over the Emerald Desert, and drifting down the Opaline River on giant lily pads, and experiencing the world's biggest sugar rush at that place where they let you bathe in your own tub full of melted chocolate."

"I'm sorry, they let you do *what*?" Em asked, her eyes growing wide in amazement.

"But just in case you do need help," Vi said to Em, "you've got the flare charm."

As Em took another step up the stony hillside, she absently lifted one hand to her chest where a simple orange pendant hung from a chain beneath her T-shirt. All she had to do was squeeze it tightly while uttering a single word, and an emergency flare would go off wherever Vi happened to be. "Did Vi and Ryn seriously not tell you what happened?" she asked Tilly.

"No. I mean, they mentioned a fire and a break-up, but that was it. They said it wasn't their place to share details or something like that."

A hint of a smile touched Em's lips. She appreciated her parents' discretion. *Her parents!* Even after all these months, there were still moments when it struck her as equally strange and incredible to be able to call them that. "It's just … it's too embarrassing," she told Tilly, lowering her hand to her side and staring out across the Topaz Sea. If she focused on a spot somewhere in the distance, it was easier to forget just how high up she was.

"I'm the queen of embarrassing moments," Tilly said. "I once skidded onto a theater stage in the middle of an opera performance, collided with the singer, and then fell off the end of the stage into the orchestra pit. And another time, I was sneaking across a roof that was seriously lacking in structural integrity, and I crashed right through it into a cozy candlelit dinner scene where a woman was down on one knee about to propose."

"Okaaaaay …"

"So whatever is so 'embarrassing' about your break-up with Dash, I'm not going to judge."

Em rolled her eyes and sighed. If she was honest with herself, she *wanted* to talk about Dash. He was never far from her mind, despite constantly reminding her brain to side-step all thoughts of him. "Fine." She cleared her throat and stared determinedly ahead as she continued walking. "Everything was great. We were really happy. And then … he said … 'I love you.'"

A beat of silence passed as Em refused to look at Tilly. Then: "I don't get it. He said 'I love you,' and you threw fire at him?"

"I didn't *throw fire* at him. I … freaked out a little bit. I said some stuff. Then Dash said some stuff. Then we were both yelling. There was obviously some unintentional magic released in the heat of the moment, and … well, neither of us was actually looking at the pavilion, so we didn't realize it was on fire until we'd finished shouting at each other." She dared a sideways glance and saw Tilly nodding slowly.

"Right. Okay. Was it your Griffin Ability? Did you tell something to start burning?"

"No. It must have been some escaped magic. You know, from … heightened emotion? And not being able to control it properly?"

Tilly nodded again. "So it was probably both of you."

"I don't know. Maybe."

"So where's the embarrassing part?"

Em raised a brow in an are-you-serious kind of way. "That bit where I majorly overreacted to three simple little words?"

Tilly gave her a knowing look. "I guess they weren't that simple."

Em released another sigh and kicked a stone out of her path. "I guess they weren't."

"So, to summarize," Tilly said, "your boyfriend told you he loves you—"

"Yes."

"—which resulted in the two of you breaking up—"

"Yes."

"—and now you're happier than you were before?"

"No! I miss him! I never wanted to break up!"

"So … the two of you should have a *conversation*—" Tilly said this last bit slowly and deliberately, like it was the most obvious thing in the world "—and then everything will be fine."

"I know, but we said some terrible things to each other, and then he stormed off, and I wouldn't be surprised if he's rethinking the whole 'I love you' thing. It probably just slipped out in the moment, and I'm guessing he very quickly realized he didn't mean it."

"I'm no expert, but I don't think *guessing* is the best way to fix a relationship problem."

"I know! I'm just … I'm scared I'm going to mess things up even more when I eventually do talk to him."

"Well," Tilly said with a shrug, "sounds like things are messed up already, so how much worse can they get?" Em directed a raised eyebrow at Tilly, who quickly added, "Okay, probably best not to answer that."

"I'm planning to talk to him as soon as we get back," Em continued, looking up and seeing that they were almost at the top of the hill, "but I end up with major anxiety every time I try to figure out exactly what I should say to him and how to explain myself, so then I just shove it all to the back of my mind and try to ignore it."

"Helpful."

"I know."

"Okay, pretend I'm Dash. What do you want to say to me?"

"I'm so not doing that."

"Come on, let's workshop this thing."

"I am not workshopping my relationship problems."

"It'll be so much fun! I mean helpful. It'll be so helpful. Just … say what you're feeling. Tell him the truth. That's all you can—Oh. Wow."

Tilly stopped abruptly as they crested the top of the hill. Em came to a halt a moment later, her eyes landing on the object they'd climbed all this way to find: the book. Made entirely of stone and roughly the size of a double garage, it looked more like a weather-worn sculpture than a literary work.

Tilly cocked her head to the side. "That's … a lot bigger than I was expecting."

"That's … an understatement."

"Well. I guess I won't be taking it back home with me."

CHAPTER 4

As the pinky purple of twilight colored the sky, and the quiet chirp of nixles filled the air, Violet Larkenwood climbed the steps carved into the side of the tree that held her home in its giant branches. She kept going, past the other small houses nestled among the upper branches, until she'd climbed as high as she could go. There, sitting on a smooth, curved section of a wide branch with a view over most of the oasis, was Ryn.

He looked up and smiled at her. "Hey. Did you see the letter? I left it out for you on the kitchen table."

"The one from the new Head Councilor?" Vi asked as she settled beside him.

"Are there any other potentially life-changing letters addressed to both of us that I should know about?"

She laughed and gave his arm a small shove. "Filigree was sleeping on it—super grumpy when I tried to move him—but yeah, I saw it and I read it."

He wrapped an arm around her and pulled her against his side. "And what do you think?"

"I don't know …" Vi rested her head on his shoulder. Though she'd already heard about most of the Guild's changes from Perry, the letter had gone into more detail about the new policies regarding Griffin Gifted fae, and exactly how the changes were being implemented.

Though the Griffin List still existed, and the Guild still required that those born with additional magical abilities be registered, they were no longer tracking Griffin Gifted fae. Anyone previously tagged had been asked to visit a Guild to have their tag enchantment removed.

And in an even bigger move, faeries with Griffin Abilities were now allowed to train and work as guardians. Any Gifted guardian would be paired with a non-Gifted guardian, and everyone was now required to wear tracker bands while working—similar to the type trainees wore during assignments so that mentors could follow what they were doing and grade their performances.

Those who had been working as guardians and were forced to leave the Guild when all Griffin Gifted fae were revealed years ago were now being contacted—if possible—and offered interviews and possible employment. Vi and Ryn fell into this latter category.

Though no formal offer had been made, the new Head Councilor had invited the two of them to the Creepy Hollow Guild for a 'discussion.' She'd mentioned that while she wasn't aware of precisely what their Griffin Abilities were, her research suggested that both Violet and Oryn Larkenwood had been dedicated, highly skilled guardians during their time and could prove to be valuable assets to the Guild should they decide to work there again.

"I respect the new Council," Vi said, "and I appreciate the changes they've made. I think they're doing excellent work now. I just ... I don't know if I'm ready to go back there. I don't know if I ever will be. And even though the tone of the letter is friendly, and it sounds as though they're open to working with us, there's the requirement for us to first submit to a truth potion and detail all our activities since we left the Guild. Which, you know ..."

"Haven't always been in line with the Law?" Ryn finished, a wry edge to his voice.

"Exactly. I don't know what kind of repercussions there might be for some of our actions."

Ryn sighed. "I know. Understandable that they would have that requirement, given that we basically headed up the entire Griffin rebel movement, and they're well aware of that. But it does make me uncomfortable."

"Yeah. We've promised privacy and safety to a lot of people, and I wouldn't want all that sensitive information to be laid bare for a Guild Council that might not remain as magnanimous as the one that's just been voted in."

"My thoughts exactly," Ryn said. "I certainly don't want them to know about *this*." He gestured to the scenery around them. "The oasis. Our hideout from the rest of the world. Oh, and what was that vague line about there being no record of us ever having our guardian markings deactivated?"

Vi rolled her eyes. "*Obviously* we never had our markings deactivated. We were too busy fleeing along with anyone else who'd just been revealed as a Griffin Gifted guardian. She knows that. I think that line was her subtle way of reminding us that we've been using our guardian weapons illegally all this time. I'm guessing that if we go there and have this 'discussion' with her and then decide *not* to work with the Guild, she won't let us leave without first deactivating our marks."

"Yeah," Ryn said. He reached for Vi's hand and rubbed his thumb over the dark, swirling patterns on the inside of her wrist. "I think you're right. And I've become quite attached to mine over the years. Something tells me you have too."

Vi let out a quiet laugh. "That's an understatement. My weapons are like an extension of my own body." With a sigh, she looked away from the markings that defined so much of who she was and cast her gaze out over the oasis. "We've done so much good here. Possibly more good than we could have achieved at a Guild. And that lifestyle ... the pace ... remember how much we worked? We hardly had time for anything else. I don't want that kind of life again."

Ryn ran his fingers lightly up and down her arm as he bent his head to press a kiss to her temple. "I'm glad we're on the same page," he murmured. "You know I'd never stop you if you wanted to go back there, but ... I'm relieved you don't. I feel like we just got our family back together. And this is our home. I don't want to change that."

"Yeah." Vi inhaled deeply and let out a happy sigh. "Sometimes I still can't believe we found her. I'm afraid it's all been a dream, and I'm going to wake up any second and find that she was never real."

Ryn's arm tightened around her. "It's real. I promise."

They sat in silence for a while, Ryn's head resting against hers, the evening sky growing darker, and glow-bugs appearing to illuminate the dusk. Vi tried to imagine what Em and Tilly might be up to right now, anticipation buzzing through her veins at the thought that this time tomorrow, her family would be complete again.

"You're excited," Ryn said quietly, and Vi could hear the smile in his voice.

"Yes." She couldn't help the grin that stretched her lips.

"Your excitement is basically blotting out every other emotion I could possibly feel right now."

Vi tilted her head up and met his gaze. "You're welcome."

He laughed. "I'm excited too, even without the overwhelming emotion you're broadcasting right now."

"It's just ... this past month has felt like years. We shouldn't have suggested she go for so long. What was I thinking? I must have been crazy. And you just *let* me insist that she take a break from everything!"

"I almost didn't. It was on the tip of my tongue to ask if you were just a tiny bit crazy. Part of me wanted to tag Em with a tracking charm and never let her leave the oasis. But ..."

"But we never wanted to be smothering, overprotective parents," Vi finished with a sigh. "Even after ..."

"Even after losing her for eighteen years. And then almost losing her again. And you were right that she needed a break. She's been far too busy since she joined us here, hurrying from one thing to the next to the next, like she's trying to make up for all the years in this world that she missed out on."

"I may have been right, but we shouldn't have let her go with *Tilly*. She's one of the biggest risk-takers we know."

"And yet she's survived this long. She's obviously doing something right."

"I guess ..." Vi raised her hand to her mouth and chewed her thumbnail.

"What do you mean you *guess*? Has Em had to use the emergency flare charm yet?"

"Well, no, but—"

"So?"

"—but there's still time!"

"Hey, come on," Ryn said gently. "What happened?"

She frowned up at him. "What do you mean?"

"You were excited, and now you're anxious. You don't need to be anxious. Em is *fine*. You heard from her a few hours ago."

"I know, I know. It's just ..." Just what? Vi wasn't sure. All she knew was that she wouldn't be entirely at ease again until her long-lost daughter was safely back inside the oasis.

Ryn withdrew his arm from around Vi and shifted to face her, his hands moving to frame her face, his fingers threading in her hair. "How about I distract you for a while?" He pushed her hair over one shoulder to expose the side of her neck before bending to press his lips to her skin.

The anxiety tightening her stomach eased, then curled into

something entirely different. "I suppose ... that wouldn't be ... terrible," she murmured, allowing her eyes to slide shut. Ryn's lips found hers, and she was vaguely aware that they were sitting out in the open, but they were so high above all the activity, and hardly anyone else ever came all the way up—

"Hello?"

Vi pulled away from Ryn with a quiet intake of breath, throwing a glance over her shoulder in the direction of the voice.

"Oh, sorry, I—" It was Dash who stood at the top of the steps. "I'm sorry. I was looking for Em. I'll ... just ..." He pointed over his shoulder with his thumb. "I'm sorry."

Vi couldn't help laughing at his flustered response. "It's fine, don't worry about it."

"Em's getting back tomorrow," Ryn added as he stood.

"Oh." Dash's brows lowered over his eyes. An unusual look for him, Vi noted as Ryn reached for her hand and pulled her up. "I, uh, must have got the dates wrong. I thought she was supposed to return yesterday. Thought I'd give her a day or two to catch up with you guys before I ... But I shouldn't have ..." He rubbed the back of his neck. "I should have ... sent a message or something."

It was strange to see Dash looking so awkward when he was generally so at ease with everyone. Things hadn't been the same since the whole pavilion fire thing. "You're welcome to come back tomorrow and talk to her," Vi said.

Dash's frown didn't budge as he looked away "I ... don't want to ruin her first evening back with you guys."

Ruin her evening? Vi opened her mouth, then clamped it shut before she could ask if Dash was planning to officially end things with Em. She longed to know what was really going on between the two of them, but that would be prying, wouldn't it? She wasn't entirely sure. Jack hadn't yet reached his teen years, and Em had only been around a few months, so Vi was still figuring out how to be the parent of an almost-adult.

"Anyway, thanks," Dash said. "I, uh, actually have some work to get back to. And sorry again for interrupting," he added as he turned away.

"Dash—" Vi called, but he was already hurrying down the steps.

Vi's shoulders sagged as she looked at Ryn. "I shouldn't ask you what he's feeling, should I."

Ryn sighed. "I don't think I could figure it out even if I wanted to. There were far too many conflicting emotions bombarding me from his direction."

Vi reached for Ryn's hand and slipped her fingers between his. "Aren't you glad we're long past all that angsty does-he-love-me, doesn't-he-love-me stuff?"

At that, Ryn started laughing. "Don't even pretend you had to deal with that kind of angst. I told you exactly how I felt about you. You were the one who stubbornly decided you didn't want to believe me."

With an innocent smile, Vi stood on tiptoe and looped her arms around his neck. "But we figured things out in the end."

Ryn wound his arms around her waist, pulled her closer, and kissed her. "We did. And Em and Dash will figure things out too, whichever way they end up going."

CHAPTER 5

THE STONE BOOK LAY OPEN ON THE GROUND, PRESENTING two giant, solid pages for all inhabitants of the sky to see. "Looks like there are words carved onto the pages," Em said, standing on tiptoe to get a better look.

"I can't make them out from down here." Tilly moved closer, placed her hands on the surface of the stone pages, and hoisted herself up. "Hmm." She rested her hands on her hips as Em climbed up beside her. "Different language."

Em brushed dirt from her hands as she looked down at the foreign lines of text, but even as she tried to make out the first word on the left-hand page, the letters began to move. "Oh!" She took a careful step backward and balanced on the edge of the book as the letters reshuffled themselves to form familiar words.

"That's handy," Tilly said. "Must be a spell that presents the words in whatever language the reader understands. I wonder what it would have gone with if you and I didn't speak the same language." She muttered the words beneath her breath as Em's eyes followed them on the page.

Welcome, seeker,
of treasure so fine.
Read in between
the words of each line.

"Read in between ..." Em repeated slowly.

"Read between the lines," Tilly murmured. "As in ... look for an implied meaning instead of—Oh," she finished just as Em blurted out, "No, that's not it."

"*Literally* read in between the lines," Tilly said.

"Yes." Em knelt on the giant stone page to peer more closely at the markings etched between the oversized lines of text. They were tiny words, easy to miss while focusing on the larger letters, but obvious enough once she realized they were there.

"That was pretty easy to figure out," Tilly said, moving to stand beside Em. "'The dragon's treasure,'" she read out loud as Em leaned forward to trace the words with one finger, "'traveled with him at all times, in the highest room of the tallest tower, where nothing but his thoughts could ever touch it.' Huh. Okay."

Em sat back on her heels and re-read the words in her head.

The dragon's treasure traveled with him at all times,
in the highest room of the tallest tower,
where nothing but his thoughts
could ever touch it.

"I'll admit," Tilly said, "I was expecting a slightly more precise location than—" She let out a yelp as the stone shifted beneath them. Em barely had time to suck in a gasp before the stone page vanished completely. Her body dropped into the darkness, leaving her stomach somewhere above her, and then pain was suddenly slicing at her as she fell between tangled twigs and razor-sharp leaves and overgrown blue flowers until—

Wham!

She hit the ground so hard that all the air was knocked instantly from her lungs. Pain radiated throughout her body as she struggled to draw a breath, to blink, to understand what the heck had just happened.

It was a forest, dark and unfamiliar, and her head was spinning, and the flowers seemed to glow, and somehow, oddly, just as everything began to fade to black, she thought she heard Dash's voice.

* * *

Em floated along a river of dreams, staring at the stars above as water lapped against her body. Then she was sitting on the pavilion steps inside the oasis, her gaze still pointed toward a starry sky. Dash was beside her, one step down, his arm wrapped loosely around her leg as he pointed out a constellation for her.

She didn't remember anything about the constellation, but she remembered the way his hand moved absently along her leg as he shifted slightly away from her, still pointing out specific patterns in the night sky. The way his fingers trailed along her skin until his hand rested against her calf.

Then they were walking, hand in hand, and Dash said something that made her laugh. In the dream, she couldn't remember what it was, couldn't make out his words, but she remembered the ache in her stomach. The ache from laughing so hard she could barely breathe. The warmth that wanted to burst from her chest. The tingle of magic weaving its way between their interlocked fingers.

Dash stopped. He turned to face Em, and his eyes were a dazzling green as he raised his other hand to tuck her hair behind her ear. "I love you."

Em froze. Then she started laughing again. "I—you—oh, you're …" She trailed off as she realized he wasn't laughing. "You don't *love* me," she blurted out before she could stop herself, still half laughing. "You haven't known me nearly long enough."

Dash cocked his head to the side, looking a little confused. "I've known you since we were children."

"Okay, yes, but you haven't really *known* me until recently."

"I … think I have."

"Um, no." There was still laughter in Em's voice, but it had an edge of panic to it now.

"Why are you arguing with me? This is the way I feel. You can't *argue—*"

"I'm saying you only *think* you feel this way."

"Okay, I …" A frown furrowed Dash's brow as he released her hand. "I'm sorry. I shouldn't have said anything. Let's just … pretend I didn't. If you're not ready for—"

"Oh, this is *my* problem? Because I'm the one who's not ready?"

"No, Emmy, I'm not saying there's a *problem—*"

"The problem is *you*, saying things you shouldn't be saying." The words came out far harsher than she intended, and the look on Dash's face told her she may as well have slapped him. "I—I mean … tonight was perfect. Why did you have to ruin it?" Crap, that sounded terrible too.

"Ruin it? I didn't think *love* was something that ruined relationships."

"Well maybe it does!" Em retorted, not even fully aware of what she meant by that.

Dash folded his arms over his chest. "So you don't think you'll ever love me?"

"I … I don't …" She honestly didn't know. She had never stopped to figure out if she should put a label on her feelings for him.

"I see. Well, good thing we figured this out before one of us fell in love. Oh wait. No. That already happened."

Em took a step back, surprised at the bitterness in Dash's tone.

This wasn't like him at all, this dry, sarcastic humor. And it was all her fault. "I ... I mean ... maybe it was never ..." Her voice wobbled. "Maybe it was never going to work out."

"Are you kidding me?" he shouted. "We just had the best evening—you just called it *perfect*—and now you're telling me it was never going to work out between us? Don't lie to me, Em. That's not what's really going on here."

The instinct to defend herself rose automatically. A match striking. A fire igniting. "Maybe it was never going to work out because of *you*," she snapped. "You don't ever take anything seriously. Everything's a great big joke to you—"

"Well someone has to balance out your eternal pessimism and sarcastic—"

"I'm not like that anymore! I'm ... freaking sunshine and puppies!"

"You are the dark cloud raining on everyone's—"

"You and your stupid, made-up F-bombs that *no one* thinks are funny—"

"You want to tell me this isn't working out because of *me*?" he interrupted. "What about you, Em? For *years* I've had to put up with you being selfish and mean—"

"I was protecting myself."

"I KNOW! But you don't have to do that anymore!"

"YES I DO!"

Dash stared at her, his lips parted, whatever words he'd been about to shout dying on his tongue. He was breathing too hard, and so was Em, as if they'd both been running.

She was about to turn, about to flee the truth she'd stumbled into, when the crackle of flames suddenly reached her ears. She whipped around, fear pounding in her chest. Burning heat, blazing light, acrid smoke—

"Em!" Her eyes darted toward the running figures just as they reached her. Vi and Ryn. "What happened?" Vi asked, breathless. "Are you okay?"

"I ... I ..." Em shook her head, her throat too tight for her to speak. She hated, *hated* this. She'd come so far in recent months, but it still felt as though it went against everything in her nature to be vulnerable in front of other people.

She glanced around, but Dash had disappeared. Had he left? Was he helping to put out the fire? The fire, crap! It was her fault. She had to—

"Em?" Vi asked, reaching for Em's shoulder.

She swallowed the tears down as best she could and forced herself to speak instead of shutting down and fleeing. "I ... um ... we were talking, and then Dash told me ..." She wrung her hands and took another breath. "That he loves me ... and then I kind of freaked out, and ... I guess I accidentally started a fire while we were fighting."

She didn't miss Ryn's raised brows, or the way he glanced at Vi, or his soft "Definitely your daughter." But then he stepped closer and pulled Em into a hug before she could say anything else, and it was far more comfort than she deserved after the damage her uncontrolled magic was currently wreaking on the pavilion.

"I—need to help," she said as Ryn hurried away to help the silhouetted figures already dealing with the fire. Water arced through the air from all directions.

"It's fine," Vi said, wrapping an arm around her. "There are plenty of people already—"

"I'm going to help," Em insisted, stepping out of Vi's grip and heading closer to the blazing pavilion, hands already rising. Her Griffin Ability was nowhere to be found at that moment, because of course that would be far too convenient, and she wasn't supposed to be using it anyway. But she knew the spell to produce water, and so she kept her hands raised and tried to focus as she stuttered over the words she'd been taught. It didn't work the first time, so she tried again, almost stumbling backward as her magic shot away from her in the form of water.

She got her breathing under control as the fire slowly died and the argument played on repeat inside her head. She had to apologize. She had to say *something*. She thought she saw Dash's tall frame through the smoke a few times, and she did her best to convince herself that she was brave enough to talk to him, but by the time the smoke and flames were gone, he was nowhere to be found.

CHAPTER 6

EM BLINKED. THEN BLINKED AGAIN, MORE FORCEFULLY THIS time, determined to shove away her half-formed dreams and remain conscious. It was easier to breathe now that she was no longer winded, but pain still echoed in waves throughout her body. Tiny creatures with wings made of light danced across her vision. She allowed her gaze to follow them as she gathered the strength to sit up.

"Don't worry, it'll be quick." It was Dash's voice again, reaching out of her dreams and into the real world. "Yeah, cool, see you tomorrow."

Strange. What kind of place was this that it could make dream voices sound like reality? Em pushed herself to her feet, almost groaning out loud at the aches and bruises. A sharp throbbing pain drew her attention to her jaw. She raised her hand and gingerly pressed the skin below her right cheek. It stung beneath her touch, and she pulled her hand away quickly. By the glowing light of the enormous blue flowers surrounding her, she saw blood on her fingertips.

"Wonderful," she murmured. Hopefully it was just a bad scratch.

She turned slowly, taking in the tangled branches, the spongy crunch of dead leaves beneath her shoes, the damp, earthy smell. One moment she'd been kneeling on top of a magical stone book, and the next thing she knew, she was falling through it into a forest. Was this forest *inside* the island? Had she fallen into the interior of the hill?

"Okay, I'll check before I leave."

New sounds reached Em's ears. The crack of a branch, the swift crunch-crunch of someone walking across the leafy forest floor. She spun around toward the source of the sound, shrinking beneath the shadow of a particularly large leaf. But it was impossible to hide herself completely, and though it was dark, the flowers and winged creatures provided enough illumination that there was no way—

A figure swept a leafy branch aside, stepped into view, and crouched down to pick something up. He straightened—and stopped. An instant later, a crossbow made of glittering gold shimmered in his hand, pointed directly at her.

No. It can't be.

Surprise and joy collided within her. "Dash?"

He froze. "Em?" He peered through the darkness at her, his expression one of disbelief. The weapon vanished. "Is that you?"

"Dash," she repeated in a whisper, her heart thudding as she realized he was real. It slammed into her then, the sudden and undeniable awareness of just how much she'd missed him. It was an actual ache at the core of her being. She wanted to throw her arms around him, kiss him, feel his strong arms pull her close. But she held herself back. Obviously. After the things she'd said to him the last time they were together, he probably never wanted to touch her again. "What—what are you doing here?" she asked.

"I'm working. What are you doing here? I thought you were on the other side of the world with Tilly."

"I'm ... I don't know." Okay, so clearly she hadn't fallen into the interior of the island. "I fell through a book, and then I ... landed here? And of all the people I could possibly run into, it had to be you."

A dozen emotions flickered across Dash's face before his expression closed off. "An unfortunate coincidence, trust me. I'll be out of your way as soon as I—"

"No!" she said. "I'm glad you're here. I ... I'm ..." And then she couldn't for the life of her figure out what else to say, so she simply repeated, "I'm glad you're here."

He hesitated before answering. "You are?"

She nodded vigorously, taking a step toward him. She hadn't planned to move—she figured he'd probably prefer to keep some distance between them—but it was as if a magnetic pull drew her closer.

"Your face," Dash said the moment she stepped out from beneath the overhang of the leaf. He crossed the distance between them, his frown deepening. "What happened? Are you okay?"

Em blinked, a little taken aback by the level of concern in his voice. "I—don't know. I fell through the trees. I think. Maybe it was a branch?" She pointed to the right side of her face. "I can just feel the one cut on this—"

"Your face is covered in scratches." He moved even closer, one hand rising toward her face, but he caught himself before he could touch her. His hand clenched briefly before he lowered it to his side.

The ache in Em's chest intensified. "Well, um ... they should heal soon, right? I'm sure it's nothing serious."

He nodded. "They should heal quickly. But that one ..." His gaze moved to her jaw again. "Does it hurt?"

She shrugged, then decided to go with the truth. "Yeah, it's stinging like a motherf—um ... frisbee?" she finished lamely.

At that, Dash's lips twitched in an almost-smile. "Let me help you," he said quietly, raising both hands. This time, he didn't stop himself. His fingers touched her jaw on either side of her face, gentle but sure. His gaze traveled her face—avoiding her eyes—as Em felt a kind of tingling warmth seep into her skin. Slowly, the slicing pain below her cheek dulled, until eventually it disappeared completely.

"All gone," Dash murmured, his thumb delicately brushing her cheek and his eyes finally meeting hers for a moment. Em wondered if she might stop breathing altogether. Then he lowered his hands and looked away, inhaling deeply before taking a step back. "What happened?" he asked again. "Where's Tilly? What did you mean about falling through a book?"

Em briefly explained the airborne islands and the enchanted stone book. "I don't know what happened to Tilly. I'm pretty sure she fell through the book with me, but when I landed here, I was alone."

"Weird," Dash said, slipping a hand into his jacket pocket and removing his amber and stylus. "I'll ask Calla to check in with her. Find out where she is and if she needs help." He scribbled across the amber's surface, then returned it to his pocket. "Do you, um, need help getting back home?"

"I …" Em trailed off. She honestly hadn't considered yet what her next step should be. "Right. Yes, you're right. I should probably return home instead of trying to get back up to that island where I might fall through something again or end up eaten by a giant spider." Dash's eyebrows jumped. She hadn't mentioned the spider creatures when explaining what had happened. "Never mind," she added quickly. "Um, didn't you say you were working? I don't want to interfere with—"

"It's fine, I'm finished. Benji already headed home, and I was taking a minute or two to fix my shoe, which ended up half-melted when it was caught in a lava toad's mouth, and then—"

"A lava toad?"

"Taken care of. Don't worry. Then Benji mirror-called to ask me if I could look for his amber, which he thought he dropped here, and then ... I saw you."

Em swallowed. "Right. Okay."

"Yeah."

"Well, um ... since I'm here, and you're here," Em said slowly, "maybe we should ... talk?"

Dash's expression grew guarded once more, but he said, "Yeah, we probably should."

"I, uh ..." She wrapped her arms around herself, took a deep breath, and decided to start with the most important bit: "I'm sorry. I'm so, so sorry. I didn't mean any of the horrible things I said. I ..." She lifted her shoulders, her thoughts floundering as she tried to figure out how to explain herself and how to fix the mess she'd made.

Say what you're feeling. Tell him the truth.

Of course she wanted to tell him the truth, but what *was* the truth? What *did* she feel? Why was it so difficult to put this into words? "I ... I missed you," she said simply. "I really missed you, Dash. I never wanted us to break up. I *want* to be with you, and I *want* to see where this goes, but 'love' felt like this huge thing I wasn't ready for, and suddenly ... in the moment ... it felt like all or nothing. And I felt ..." She waved her hands, still struggling to find the right words.

"Cornered? Trapped? Pressured into saying the same thing?"

"Yes. All of those things. And ..."

"And?" he prompted gently when she didn't go on.

"Scared," she admitted quietly. "I was scared. I'm still scared."

"Why, Emmy?" Dash moved closer and took both her hands in his. "What are you scared of? Why do you feel like you need to protect yourself from *me*?"

"Because I—like you—a lot—and ..." Her words were becoming more stilted as emotion thickened her voice. She tried to blink her tears away, tried to get herself under control. She cleared her throat and took another breath. "And I'm happy. I'm really happy. With *everything* in my life. And that means I'm going to lose it all." The truth tumbled out of her before she had time to comprehend it. But there it was, and suddenly, it made a lot of sense. She'd had good things snatched away from her time and time again during her eighteen years, and now that she finally had everything she wanted, a part of her didn't believe it would last.

Instead of responding, Dash pulled Em against his chest and wrapped both arms around her. Her eyelids slid shut, and a long sigh shuddered past her lips. "You're not going to lose it all," Dash said into her hair. "You're vastly underestimating your family if you think they'll ever let you go. You've already seen that. And as for you and me ..." He released her and moved back, just far enough that Em could see his face, his intense gaze, his earnest expression. He lifted one hand and brushed his thumb across her cheek again. "I want to be with you, Em. It's as simple as that. But I can't promise you that it will never end. I don't *want* it to end. I don't *plan* for it to end. But I can't see the future, so I don't know what will happen. That's the risk we choose to take if we want to see where this goes."

She took a deep breath and nodded. "I know." It was terrifying, and a tiny part of her still screamed that it was safer to back off now and end things. Protect her heart. But the part of her that had missed him every day, the part that almost exploded with happiness at the first sight of him this evening—even with a weapon pointed straight at her—knew better. That part of her knew he was worth the risk.

"And I'm really sorry too," Dash added, "for all the things we shouted at each other. For all the things *I* said. You're not eternally pessimistic, and you're not a dark raincloud. I was just ... I was hurt, and I lashed out, and I'm sorry."

"It's okay, I know you didn't mean those things. Or at least ... I really, really hoped you didn't. Part of me wondered if maybe you were finally seeing the real me, and you'd decided you didn't actually, well … *love* me."

He grinned then—a genuine mischief-filled Dash grin—and Em's insides warmed at the sight. "My goodness, Emmy, that was a big, scary word you just used."

"Shut up," she mumbled, pushing his shoulder, but she couldn't fight the smile curving her lips.

"I already know the real you, Em, and I've … *cared about* you —" he emphasized those words with a knowing look "—for a long time. The past few months, I've only grown to *care about* you even more. One fight and a burned-down pavilion isn't going to change that."

She tried to fight her ridiculously large smile, but it was impossible. She was basically a beaming floodlight right now. "Can I kiss you?"

Suspicion wiped away the grin on Dash's face. "Who are you, and what did you do with the real Em? You're *never* this polite. You normally just jump out of nowhere and attack me with—"

She wrapped her arms tighter around his neck and jumped. Within a second, her legs were hooked around his waist, and his arms were secure around her back, holding her close as he laughed. She angled her head down and kissed him. His laughter vanished as something else took over, and he returned the kiss with the fervor of one who had longed for water and was finally allowed to drink. His fingers dug into her back, and the way his lips moved against hers was so familiar and so *right* and flip, she had missed this. She had missed *him*. Never again would she be so stupid as to mess things up the way she'd—

The earth trembled beneath them, and Dash stumbled, almost losing his grip on her. "What was that?" he asked breathlessly, lowering her to her feet.

"I … I don't … Oh, crap, maybe it's the same magic that

dropped me here in the first—" Em gasped as some invisible forced ripped her clear out of Dash's arms. "Dash—" she said, but it was the only word she managed to get out before swirling darkness encompassed everything and the earth dropped away beneath her feet.

CHAPTER 7

Em fell out of the air and watched the solid stone book fly up to meet her. Something jerked her to an almost-halt before lowering her the final distance, so at least she didn't land as painfully this time.

"Em!" Em raised her head and looked around to see Tilly hurrying toward the book. She stood and scrambled to the edge of the stone page as quickly as possible, reaching for Tilly's outstretched hand. "Ohthankthepunch," Tilly said as Em jumped down. Tilly dragged her several paces away before letting go.

"Thank the *what*?" Em asked. Then she shook her head. "What happened? Where did you go?"

"I ... um ..." For once, Tilly seemed at a loss for words. She cleared her throat, then asked, "Where did *you* go?"

"I—" Em's face heated at the memory of the scene she'd been plucked from. "Dash," she said simply.

Tilly nodded slowly, her gaze becoming unfocused. "Okay. Makes sense."

"It does? I thought we were treasure hunting, and the next thing I know I'm falling right through a solid stone book and landing in an entirely different part of the world. Where there was no treasure, by the way." Though in Em's opinion, what she'd found had been far better than treasure.

"The treasure …" Tilly's gaze was still directed somewhere past Em, her expression thoughtful. "I don't think it's the kind of treasure we were thinking of."

Em narrowed her eyes, her mind working. "Where exactly did you go, Tilly?"

"I …" Tilly's lips pulled into a small smile as her cheeks flushed. "I'm not going to say."

"Oh, *now* you don't feel like talking?"

"My point," Tilly continued, "is that I think the 'treasure' is the thing or person that's been occupying our minds the most." She gestured at the magical stone book but made no move to approach it. "The poem or riddle or whatever it is says the dragon's treasure travels with him at all times. That nothing but his thoughts can touch it."

"It also says something about the highest room of the tallest tower."

"Maybe that's the dragon's head. The treasure—the thing that's on his mind the most—is in his head, which is where nothing but the rest of his thoughts can touch it."

"Maybe … I guess …" Em considered Tilly once again. "So who were you transported to? Who exactly has been on *your* mind all this time?"

"I … would prefer not to talk about that."

"Wow."

Tilly folded her arms over her chest and attempted to look stern. "Don't 'wow' me, little miss."

Em mirrored her stance, arms across her chest. "You seem to be having some feelings about this. We should workshop them. It'll be fun. I mean helpful. It'll be—" A shudder rippled through the ground, almost knocking Em off her feet. She threw her arms out to balance herself. "What the heck was that?"

"I don't know."

Em looked around as the island began to tremble. It seemed, impossibly, that it was beginning to change shape. Her gaze caught on a section of rocky ground near the bottom of the hill, where loose stones were running down the incline and falling off the island. Then she looked a little further and saw—No. That wasn't possible. Her mind instantly rejected what her eyes seemed to be seeing: A rocky wing-shape unfurling itself.

Em ran around the stone book and looked down the other side of the hill, and—yep. There it was. Another suspiciously dragon-like wing. "No way, no way," she muttered as she spun around and ran another few paces—but there it was. A great big head made of crumbling stone, stretching away from the base of the hill. "This isn't an island." She whirled back around, her gaze landing on Tilly. "This is an actual dragon."

"Yeah. I just figured that out. Crapazoid," she muttered at the same time Em gasped, "Fuzz-knuckle." Which, some vague part of her mind registered, Dash would have appreciated.

A violent shiver traveled through the island, and this time Em found herself flat on her backside. Then the ground tipped side-ways, and suddenly she was rolling. Over and over and over, stones bumping her head and face, and digging into her body from all sides. Then she jerked to a stop and began rolling back, seemingly uphill, which must mean the dragon was banking the other way now.

Em's hands fumbled with the chain at her neck, and the moment she got the pendant free, she gripped it as hard as if her life depended on it—which it probably did—and uttered the single word Vi had made her practice multiple times. There was too much going on for her to tell whether it flashed or heated up or—

"Oh!" She groaned out loud as she smacked into the side of the stone book.

"Em!" Tilly shouted, scrambling toward her. Her face was scratched and dirty. "You okay?"

"I—I think so." The rocking motion seemed to have stopped for now, so at least they weren't about to fly off the dragon's back.

"Okay," Tilly said as she sat up, keeping a firm grip on Em's arm. "Step number one: don't panic."

"Uh huh." Em nodded as she tried to catch her breath.

"Step number two: when we get off this flying dragon island—because we *will* get off it—do not tell Vi about this part."

"Um … I may have already activated the flare charm."

"*What?* Ugh, come on! Your parents are *never* going to let me live this down!"

"Do you think Vi will be able to find us?"

"Unless we're magically concealed by something I don't know about, yes, she should find us very quickly."

"No faerie paths though," Em said. "It'll take them a while to—"

"Trust me, she'll be back with Bandit or one of the gargoyles or a flying carpet before you can say, 'Hey, Mom! It wasn't Tilly's fault!'"

"Uh huh. Okay."

"Because that's exactly what you're going to say, right?"

"Right," Em answered, but she was distracted by the rising and falling of the dragon's wings and the rocking motion of the island-that-wasn't-an-island.

"Let me … just …" Tilly reached for her pants pocket, then put a hand out to brace herself as the dragon dipped a little to the side before righting itself again. She pulled out her amber and stylus, let go of Em's arm, and began to write a message. "Oh!" The dragon swooped again, and both Em and Tilly slammed up against the edge of the stone book. "Well, there goes my amber," Tilly said, and Em watched it tumble away and out of sight.

"I have mine," she said, managing to wedge it free of her back pocket as the dragon returned to its normal flying pattern. "It's—oh." Em's heart fell at the sight of the crack running down the middle of her amber. "I must have landed on it." She frowned at the device. "I'm still fairly new to this magical stuff. Does a crack mean it won't work?"

"Depends on the crack." Tilly took the amber from her. "Looks like this one's gone almost all the way through. Definitely won't work anymore. But don't worry, I managed to send a half-written, only partially cryptic message to Vi. I'm sure she'll figure it out. In the meantime, let's make sure we can't be thrown clear of this great, stone beast." She let go of Em again and reached for the charm bracelet around her wrist. The little metal shapes that hung from it were hollow, and each contained important items she might need while out on an expedition—like the non-slip gloves she'd given Em earlier.

With deft fingers, she removed one of the charms, opened it, and pulled out what looked like little more than a thread with … was that a minuscule anchor on the end? Em couldn't quite tell. After returning the charm to the bracelet, Tilly enlarged the item to reveal that it was actually a length of rope with a grappling hook on the end. With a burst of magic, the hook shot away from her and embedded itself in the hard, stony surface of the dragon's back. "Right," she said, wrapping the end of the rope around one hand and grabbing hold of Em with the other. "We're not going anywhere until the rescue party shows up."

CHAPTER 8

CALLA'S HEART SEEMED TO SIMULTANEOUSLY LODGE ITSELF IN her throat and plummet all the way to the base of the tree in the same moment. And then it took off in a gallop, pumping adrenaline through her body. She rushed to Chase's side, taking his arm to help him across the room. "What happened? Are you okay?"

"I'm fine, I'm fine," he mumbled, but he was limping, and he had multiple cuts on his face, and there was far too much blood drenching his clothes. He lowered himself to the floor and leaned back against the edge of the couch as Calla's mind spun back to the Seelie Court, to the morioraith, to the countless other injuries Chase had sustained in the years since she'd met him. He had survived worse than this, she reminded herself. Her heart had survived worse than this. They would both be fine, as they always were. Still, the amount of blood currently seeping into their living room rug was a little alarming.

Calla gently lifted one side of Chase's jacket. There was a hole in his T-shirt, and beneath it, a gaping wound. "That looks bad," she murmured.

"It's fine," Chase repeated, pressing the palm of hand against the injury with a grimace. "I removed the piece of metal already. I'm just losing a bit of blood while the wound heals."

"A bit?" Calla repeated. "Why did you drag yourself all the way up here instead of getting help from someone down there as soon as you reached the oasis?"

"I'm fine, Cal, it's not serious."

"You're covered in blood! There is a *hole* in your side!"

"Most of the blood isn't mine—"

"I'm finding that hard to believe."

"—and the hole will close up quickly. Besides, I didn't want help from anyone else. I just wanted to get back to you."

Calla let out an impatient breath. "Don't be a smart-ass." Then she jumped up, ran to the bathroom, and returned with a towel and a box of healing supplies. Given how often they used it, it was always within easy reach. "Here," she said, lifting his hand and pressing the rolled-up towel against the wound, then lowering his hand again. She grabbed a bottle from the box—a tonic that aided in healing—and forced him to take a swig while she dragged her finger along the T-shirt, neatly slicing through it with a tiny spark of magic. She peeled away part of the fabric and placed her hand against his skin to send some of her own magic into his body.

"None of this is necessary," Chase said as he leaned a little to the side and returned the bottle to the healing supplies box. "You know I'll be fine without—"

"If you use the word 'fine' one more time—"

"Okay," he answered, a faint smile on his lips. "I'm sorry."

Calla released a steadying breath. She'd lost count of the number of times they had done this—peeled bloodied clothes off each other, used their magic to heal each other—and though it sent her heart racing through various stages of panic every time, it also seemed kind of normal by now. But it struck her suddenly that this was the life they were bringing a ... 'bagel' into. Cold fear sent a chill through her body. What had they been thinking? They couldn't do this.

No. They *could* do this. Ryn and Vi had made it work, and she and Chase would make it work too. They had spoken about this. It had been one of their many fears. And they had promised one another that they would make whatever changes needed to be made in order for this to work.

Calla cleared the doubt from her mind and asked, "What happened?"

"An ambush. An explosion. Metal shards flying everywhere. I didn't get a shield up in time. Don't know who it was. Someone who clearly hates our newest client."

"Or someone who hates *you* if they've figured out who you are. Perhaps the whole thing was a set-up."

"Perhaps. I don't know. We did our usual background check, and nothing seemed suspicious about this woman, but we could have been wrong. Either way, we won't be working with her again. I ... I'm not even sure if she made it."

Calla was quiet for a few moments before answering. "I don't think you should try to find out," she said eventually. "In case the whole thing was a set-up."

Chase nodded. "I know. Too much of a risk." He moved his hand—the one not currently pressing a towel against his abdomen —and covered hers. "Thank you. I'm feeling better already."

"Liar."

He laughed quietly. "No, seriously, I am. You know I heal quickly." He lifted his hand away, and Calla removed hers—with some reluctance—from his skin, ending the flow of magic between them. They sat like that on the floor for another few minutes, Chase sharing more details of the meeting up until the moment of the explosion, and Calla watching the cuts on his face fade to mere scratches. Eventually he lifted the towel, and all that remained of the wound was a patch of pink skin. Well, aside from all the blood.

Calla exhaled in surprise. They had been together for years, and somehow she always underestimated the speed of his healing ability. "I told you it wasn't as bad as it looked," Chase said. "It was basically a surface wound."

"It was not a surface wound."

"Well, whatever it was, it's almost gone." He climbed to his feet, pulling Calla up with him.

"I guess you should probably shower," Calla said. "I'll get all of this—" she pointed to the rug and the edge of the couch "—cleaned up."

Chase took her hand and lifted it to his lips, pressing a kiss against the small, dark outline of a flower on her fourth finger—her very first tattoo, commemorating the first mission she'd completed after joining Chase and his team. "You don't want to join me?"

She couldn't help smiling. "In the shower?"

"Yes."

She paused, then said, "I suppose we don't really need dinner, do we?"

"Join me in the shower, and I'll help you with dinner afterwards."

She leaned forward, kissed him, and whispered, "Deal." Then she bent and closed the healing supplies box.

"Calla?" Chase asked, and there was something different in his tone.

She straightened, the box in her hands. Chase's gaze was pointed somewhere past her. "Yeah?"

"Why is there a bagel on a cake stand in the middle of the table?"

The bagel. She hadn't had time to cover it yet.

Her heart seized, all her excitement and fear and hope hitting her at once. Chase was looking at her now, his warm gaze burning into hers, and he *knew*. She could tell that he knew. It was about to explode from her, the thing she'd been dying to tell him for days—

241

But that, of course, was when the fifth thing went wrong. Outside the window, orange light blazed so brightly that Calla squinted as it flooded into their living room. A moment of silence passed as her brain worked through a dozen possibilities, and then suddenly, she realized what had caused the light. "The flare charm. Em's emergency flare charm."

CHAPTER 9

THE BRIGHT FLARE OF LIGHT WAS ACCOMPANIED BY A PAINFUL tug at the center of Vi's chest. She had cast the enchantment to do exactly that, so there would be no possible way she could miss it, no matter what she might be doing at the time. "No," she whispered, frozen for a moment as the realization sank into her bones. "This is not happening."

Then she and Ryn both jumped to their feet. Her magic pushed her faster and faster down the winding stairway, until her surroundings blurred and it was a wonder she didn't trip and tumble all the way to the bottom of the tree. She couldn't think. She was acting on instinct, the same words repeating through her brain: *Em is okay. She's okay, she's okay, she's okay.*

Vi skidded to a halt at the base of the tree, her thoughts turning for a moment to Jack—he would be climbing up to the house soon, expecting to find her there, expecting dinner to be ready soon—but he was safe here at the oasis. Someone would take care of him until she and Ryn returned. This had happened before, and he had been fine. *He will be fine.*

It was Em who might not be fine. Em who needed them right now.

She's okay. She'll be okay.

Vi would not—*could not*—consider any other possibility.

She and Ryn ran for the edge of the oasis, and at some point before reaching the layer of magic that concealed the entire place within a protective dome, Calla and Chase appeared. Vi was vaguely aware of Calla asking her if she knew where Em was, but she couldn't answer. Not yet.

Get beyond the dome. Search for Em. Then get there as quickly as possible.

She passed through the magic that kept the oasis hidden and stumbled onto the desert sand. She landed on her knees and let her eyes slide shut, reaching out for Em with her mind. *Where are you, where are you?*

She saw sky above and sea below. She saw a smooth stone surface on one side, and rocky ground beneath Em's feet. She felt a strange, slow rocking motion. With the glimpses came a sense of Em's location. Enough for Vi to direct the faerie paths. She opened her eyes.

"Did you find her?" Ryn asked immediately.

"Yes," was all Vi said. It would take precious seconds to explain, and there was no point. Not when she could simply take them there. "Follow me." She grabbed Ryn's hand and ran into the faerie paths through the doorway he'd already opened, trusting that Calla and Chase were right behind him.

They rushed out of the darkness onto a small piece of land hovering a short distance above the sea. Other islands surrounded them at different levels, some below, and some of them so high up they appeared minuscule in comparison to the one they stood one.

Vi spun on the spot, eyes darting all over the bare, rocky surface. She noticed all of a sudden that Chase's face, arms and pants were smeared with blood. Clean T-shirt, though. Strange. But whatever had happened to him, Vi couldn't let it distract her. As long as he wasn't mortally wounded, she had more important things to focus on.

The island was tiny and covered in little more than earth and loose stones, with a gentle incline rising to what could hardly be called a peak. Vi climbed quickly to the highest point, calling for both Em and Tilly. Ryn moved a few paces ahead of her, and she knew before she'd reached the top of the hill that there was nothing of interest on the other side.

"Try again," he said, turning to face her. He was familiar with her process, the way she homed in on a precise location step by step. Sometimes it took a whole string of trips through the paths, depending on how far away her starting point was.

"Yeah," Vi said, already closing her eyes again, blocking everything else out and reaching for Em. She turned again, raising her left hand. "That way," she said, her eyes blinking open as she pointed.

"Okay," Ryn said. "Back into the paths." He lifted his stylus to open a doorway.

And nothing happened.

"Oh," he said. "The paths aren't accessible here."

Vi twisted around to look past Calla and Chase back down the hill. "So we can open them down there, but not here." She looked up. "Which means they probably don't work any higher than this. Maybe that's why Em and Tilly need help. They're too high up and can't access the paths." *Please let it be that*, she thought. A problem as simple as inability to access the paths was easy for them to deal with. Although, she thought with a jolt of fear, if it were that simple a problem, wouldn't Em have sent a message instead of—

The ground beneath Vi's feet began to shudder, and she swiftly raised her arms to help maintain her balance. "A tiny island with earthquakes?" Calla asked as the tremble came to an end. "This is weird."

"We need the gargoyles," Chase said. "Or a dragon. Or both.

I'll go to the mountain and get them. They'll find Em and Tilly quickly."

"I'll go with you," Calla said. "It'll be faster if there are two of us to bring them through the paths."

"You should go too," Vi said to Ryn. "Even quicker with three."

"Will you be—"

"I'll be fine. If there's another earthquake, I'll head back down to the faerie paths. And I'll keep searching for Em. Then we know exactly which way to go when you get back."

Ryn hesitated for another beat, then nodded. "Okay."

"Thank you. Please be quick. Oh, wait—" Something vibrated against Vi's side, and she stuck her hand inside her jacket to find her amber there. She'd completely forgotten she had it on her when she'd climbed the tree earlier to find Ryn. "It's from Tilly!" She squinted at the amber's surface. In a scrawl almost too messy to read, it said:

Stone dragon island flying toward

"What?" Vi muttered. "'Stone dragon island flying toward'?"

"Clearly that's only half a message," Ryn said.

"I know, but … stone dragon island? Is that … could that be …"

The earth shook again. Almost in unison, all four of them turned their gazes down. "I really hope we're all thinking the wrong thing," Calla murmured.

"Unfortunately," Chase said, "I don't think we are." From the corner of her eye, Vi saw him reach for Calla's hand. Vi swallowed and extended her arm to find Ryn's. Beneath them, the shudder intensified.

"We need to get back down to—" Without warning, the entire island rolled to the side. "Crap!" Vi gasped a second before she hit the ground and began rolling down the hill that had suddenly become much steeper. Ryn's hand had been torn from hers as she fell, and now she scrabbled at the ground with both hands, her magic gouging holes into the rocky surface so her fingers could find purchase. Her body jerked to a halt, the palms of her hands stinging as she clung tightly to the ground. No, to the dragon. This was a *dragon*.

"Ryn!" she shouted.

"Here!" He was on her left, a little higher up, holding onto a blazing guardian dagger that was jammed into the hard, stony surface. With his free hand, he fumbled with his stylus.

"Calla?" Vi shouted.

"We're fine," Calla called from somewhere below. "Chase just opened a doorway. Meet you at the mountain?"

"Okay," Vi called back. Ryn's doorway was spreading open, and he was extending a hand toward Vi, but the heaving, rolling motion of the stone dragon creature was causing her body to swing from side to side. She took a deep breath, released one hand, and launched herself toward Ryn. He grabbed her wrist, and together they fell into the darkness.

* * *

In the end, the rescue was quick. They made it to the mountain in record time—though every passing second raised Vi's anxiety another notch—and took a dragon and three gargoyles. Once they were soaring above the Topaz Sea, weaving their wave between the airborne islands with Vi's Griffin Ability to direct them toward Em, it didn't take long to spot the exact flying island creature they were after.

And there they were, Em and Tilly, standing with legs astride while clutching a single rope, looking for all the world as if they were tandem dragon riding. Though relief was the overwhelming emotion that flooded Vi's body, there was a definite flash of pride there too. *That's my girl*, she couldn't help thinking.

Ryn and Chase directed their gargoyles to fly above Em and Tilly. Moments later, ropes dropped down toward them. One was a glittering guardian version, while the other was of the non-magical variety. Chase must have grabbed it from the caves when they got to the mountain. Em and Tilly each took hold of a rope, and seconds later, they were flying away from the stone creature.

Vi directed her dragon downward until she was flying just beneath them. She twisted around in her harness and watched as they dropped onto the dragon's back. And finally, *finally*, she released a sigh of relief. Em slid down into a sitting position behind Vi and wrapped her arms around Vi's waist. With her chin on Vi's shoulder, she said, "Thank you, thank you! I'm so sorry!"

And then they were flying through the paths and back home.

After a thousand apologies and promises to do anything Vi could possibly think of to make up for this, Tilly departed, saying there was something she needed to take care of. Vi barely had a chance to get a word in before she was gone.

They crossed the dome layer into the oasis, Em talking a mile a minute, explaining precisely what she and Tilly had been trying to do before everything went wrong, and apologizing over and over for worrying Vi. "I realize now that it was a bad idea, but I thought we were going to find *treasure*. Actual treasure. I mean ... you would have been excited by that too, right?"

"*You* are my treasure," Vi said to her, pulling her against her side and kissing her cheek. "I don't need to go hunting for more."

Em looped her arm through Vi's. Her face seemed to flush as she said, "Yeah, I think I've figured out now what real treasure is."

Ryn and Chase handed over the gargoyle and dragon reigns to Carter and Kobe, requesting they return the creatures to the mountain, and Em quietly told Vi what had happened when she fell through a magical book and found Dash on the other end. And then somehow, a short while later, they were all crowding into Vi and Ryn's living room where both Jack and Dash were anxiously waiting for them.

"*There* you are!" Dash exclaimed. "Nobody could tell me what was happening." He barely had a chance to reach for Em's hand before Jack threw himself at his sister, almost knocking her over, and begged for every detail of the Infinity Serpent. Supposedly the fae world's fastest and scariest theme park ride, it was an experience Tilly had treated Em to early in their trip.

Vi watched Em as she happily began answering her little brother's questions while stealing glances at Dash over Jack's head. It seemed things were right again between the two of them, and some tiny part of Vi that had remained tightly coiled began to ease. She gave herself a moment to breathe, to appreciate that her family was safe and complete, to give Ryn's hand a squeeze, to notice that … Calla and Chase were being … strange? They were together in a corner, and they couldn't stop hugging and kissing one another, and it seemed almost as if … were they *crying*?

Vi directed a questioning look at Ryn, but he shrugged and frowned. "Hey, are the two of you okay?" Vi called across the room.

They both nodded, but Calla was definitely wiping tears from her cheeks.

"Are you sure?" Vi asked. "Did something happen?" Something *must* have happened, given all the blood Chase was covered in. But it wasn't exactly an uncommon state for any of them, and as far as Vi could tell, he seemed fine.

"A bagel," Calla answered, her shining eyes still pinned on Chase's. It made little sense to Vi, but the way Chase smiled at her when she said this was so beautiful it sent a jolt through Vi's chest. It was clear to anyone watching that everything important to him— his 'treasure'—was standing right in front of him. Calla sniffed and laughed. "I mean a baby. A baby happened."

"A baby," Vi repeated.

"A baby?" Ryn and Dash said in unison.

"A babyyyyy!" Jack shouted.

It was Em who ran across the room first, colliding with Calla and Chase and throwing her arms around them both. Then Jack vaulted over the back of the couch, shouting, "A cousin! We're getting a cousin!" as he crashed into the three of them.

Dash let out a whoop as he hurried around the couch. "I guess it's group-hug time!"

Vi looked at Ryn, a smile growing on her lips. His shocked expression melted away, warmth reaching his eyes as he answered her smile with his own. Then Vi crossed the room, Ryn moving with her, and embraced her family.

Thank you for traveling back into the Creepy Hollow world with me! I hope you enjoyed the journey.

xx Rachel

Rachel Morgan spent a good deal of her childhood living in a fantasy land of her own making, crafting endless stories of make-believe and occasionally writing some of them down.

After completing a degree in genetics and discovering she still wasn't grown-up enough for a 'real' job, she decided to return to those story worlds still spinning around her imagination.

These days she spends much of her time immersed in fantasy land once more, writing fiction for young adults and those young at heart.

Lightning Source UK Ltd.
Milton Keynes UK
UKHW012128221121
394427UK00010B/563/J